If you purchase aware that this  "unsold and destroyed" to the publisher, and neither the author nor the publisher has received any payment for this "stripped book."

Published in 2022 by Eve Bailey

Edited by Leslie Bailey

All Images Copyright © 2022 by Eve Bailey

All rights reserved

No part of this publication may be reproduced, stored in a retrieval system, or transmitted, in any form or by any means, electronic, mechanical, photocopying, recording, or otherwise without the prior permission of the publishers.

Text copyright © 2022 by Eve Bailey

Map and illustrations © Eve Bailey

This edition first printing, May 2022

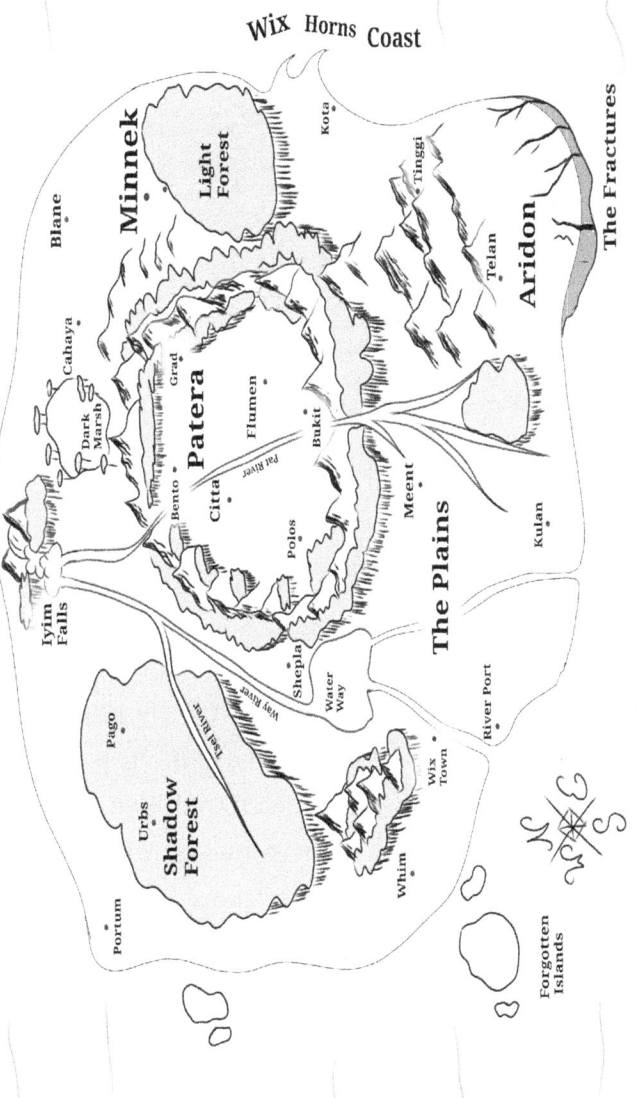

Note from the Author

You, the reader, will most likely skip this part. I know, because I have before.

But to you who decided to read it, I hope you'll give me grace. This is my first work of fantasy, and a book at that. I wouldn't be surprised if you found some mistakes in here yourself that we missed!

I worked hard on this book, this world, this continent called Iyim. I hope that you enjoy

Bonded as much as I did writing it!

In this book is a world that I would love to be apart of, a world that I would love if it was real. I hope that I can transport you there as you read.

As for acknowledgments. . . .

Thank you to my family! Mom, thank you so much for helping with editing and making this imaginative idea become reality! Thank you, Dad, for giving out ideas and advice! Thank you to my sister, Moriah, who always gives little tidbits of ideas and confidence boosts! My little brothers, Nate and Banner, the stinkers who gave me a knowing of responsibility. To know that you can't give up. And to all of my extended family and friends, there are so many I can't count, thank you all for your support, it means so much! Also, to all the people I've met on social media, thank you for your support, too! You all gave me the confidence for finishing this book and for very hopefully continuing this series!

God Bless!
-Evey

Contents:

Chapter	Page
One: A Visitor	9
Two: Gone	23
Three: Finding The Way	37
Four: Preparations	55
Five: A New Bond	65
Six: Learning	78
Seven: Reading	92
Eight: The Box	101
Nine: New Meetings	112
Ten: Racing and Fun	122
Eleven: Reviews	138
Twelve: A New journey	150
Thirteen: Attacked	165
Fourteen: Recovering and Continuing	181
Fifteen: Water Fun	197
Sixteen: Embarrassment yet Healing	213
Seventeen: The Colony	229

Eighteen: Destruction yet New Growth	242
Nineteen: Training for both Girl and Wixen	257
Twenty: Traveling to Riverport	265
Twenty one: Zerah's Advice	277
Twenty two: Visiting and Giving	290
Twenty three: Something Strange	304
Twenty four: Goodbyes and More Strangeness	315
Twenty five: An Old Friend	325
Twenty six: A New and Frightening Path	335
Epilogue	344
Index	347

ONE

A Visitor

It wasn't my fault.

Unfortunately, my stomach's at fault.

All I wanted was some food.

So I ran as fast as I could from the farmer and sentries.

The streets were filled with people, but I could still hear his screaming from behind.

Turning into an alley way dust filled my view and I coughed, but kept running.

Then people were around me again.

I spun in a circle to see him gone.

Leaning over, I breathed rapidly, then looked at my prize. A sack full of beautiful, fresh vegetables.

Closing the sack back up, I shifted through the crowd and walked to the edge of town.

A little cottage came into view and I smiled.

I stepped through the door and set the sack on the dining room table. "I'm home, Grandmother!"

Her voice came from her room, "You bought some food for dinner?"

I remembered the baker's voice in my head as I ran away, 'Get back here yeh little thievin' rat!' and grimaced. "Uh, yeah, I bought some things for dinner."

"Good!" she called, "But it's too early in the day to cook, so you don't have to start yet!"

"M'kay!" I answered, closing the door to my room.

The sun.
The sun was setting, yet again.
Like it always did at the end of the day.
I wondered if it would always come back up.

Little did I know, my life was about to change.

Little did I know that hurting is going to be apart of it.

Little did I know nothing would be the same.

I gazed out the open window and warmth of the evening sun burst upon my skin.

The birds were twittering in the trees as I watched the sun start disappearing behind the trees.

Everything was peaceful at this hour.

At rest.

Unlike earlier, but let's just pretend you didn't see that part of me.

Leaning up against the 'sill, I could see Grandmother's rose bushes brushing up against the wall.

I lived in a cottage with her in Polos, a town in the Realm of Patera. My mother died when I was born and my father disappeared not long after that, so that's why I lived there.

I know kind of sad, right? Well, I'm happy that I had my grandmother, that she took care of me. I wouldn't have it any other way.

"Please come help me with the laundry,

Eleny."

I smiled as her voice filled my ears. My grandmother had raised me, my whole sixteen and a half years of life. She was the sweetest old lady anyone would know. I knew that I was very fortunate to have someone like her to look after me.

But sometimes she puzzled me. She was so kind that she even gave things away to people who needed it, hence us being poor. Even if it was something she loved. That's what I couldn't figure out. I pushed my eyebrows together and scrunched up my nose. *Hmm.*

Grandmother's sing-song voice pulled me out of thought again, "Eleny?"

"Coming!" I jumped up and ran swiftly down the stairs, to the laundry on the clothesline out the back door. When I gathered all of the sun scented clothes, I brought them to the laundry room.

Grandmother looked up at me, her thin lips smiling. She was a little bit shorter than me, but was quite fit. Her amber eyes, the same shade as mine, sparkled. After we finished I went to the kitchen and started making dinner.

As I cooked the stew above the fire, the red

and yellow flames danced in the fireplace. Our kitchen was quite small, but there was enough room for about five Thasfaen women.

A presence suddenly entered my mind, there was a knock on the front door.

Who would come at this hour?

I went and opened the oak wood door, standing there was a Thasfaen woman with a child in her arms. My eyes went wide.

"Does F-Fenmy live here?" she shifted the boy to the other hip.

"Grandmother?" I called, shuffling my feet.

She walked up to the door, "Hello, how may I help you?" she asked the woman.

"P-please, I-I-I need help," the woman stuttered, she looked tired and weary. The little boy's pleading deep blue eyes went straight to my heart. His cheeks were smudged with dirt and his hair was knotted.

Grandmother must have seen the boy's face, too, for she welcomed them in warmly. After they both sat down in the dining room, I found some bowls and served the stew.

"My name is Palana, my baby, Omar, has magical powers, I found out when he picked up the kitchen table," the woman smiled then glanced at grandmother nervously, "Please help me, I can't give him up."

I glanced at grandmother, she looked at me with a warm, but tense, face.

There was a forced abandonment law for babies with magical powers in Patera. My Grandmother used to help smuggle them out when she was younger.

We had to help. I bit my lip and nodded at her.

She nodded back, "What about the child's father?"

Palana sniffed, new tears coming forth, "He wants nothing of him. He was going to give him to the soldiers, that's why I escaped."

"Where did you live?" Grandmother took a sip of the stew.

"In Bukit, near the river." She gave her child a bite of carrots, "My mother told me that you could help, I have been traveling all day."

"Then we shall leave tonight, as soon as possible," Grandmother's lips turned up a tiny bit.

"Thank you!" said Palana, as she looked down at the boy and squeezed him tight against her chest, rocking him back and forth.

The next hour grandmother started making plans with the Thasfaen woman while I packed food.

I stepped outside, the cool breeze greeted me and the oak trees did as well. The sun had set but I could still see, walking to the cellar. The cellar was only a few feet away from the door so it only took me about seven steps.

Yep, I was short.

I opened the hatch and lit a lamp inside, it was getting darker. When I finished packing the food, I went back to the house and set the bag on the table.

I then went to sit on the floor to play with the boy. Eventually the child came and fell asleep in my lap. With curly, soft blond hair, and a small, stubby nose, he gave a little snore. He was a beautiful little boy, just around two years old.

Why would they want to be rid of this little one? He is just different from them, I thought.

Since he was calmly asleep, I took him to my room and put him on my bed. When I came back to the dining room I looked at the map they had laid out.

"We need to get to the tunnels and go in, turn left, then right, and walk straight the rest of the way," my grandmother informed, "Then, when we reach the other side, we go down this road that leads to Shepla."

While studying the map, another presence came, apart from my grandmother and the Thasfaen.

Someone knocked at the door.

I bit my lip and scowled. *Another one? Hey everybody, we're open all night! Come at any time!* But I shook that thought away. If someone needed help, we would help.

Grandmother walked to the door and went outside.

Palana and I sat, silently waiting. I focused on the Thasfaen, her hair was chestnut and was covering some of her oval face. Her dark green eyes were big and round, probably from nervousness.

Almost a half hour later the door opened, which let in a draft that made me shiver. My grandmother slid back in with a grave face.

Oh no, did someone find out? Did somebody see the child and told the soldiers? My mind raced, thinking about all of the possibilities of what could have made grandmother look so grave. She took me to her bedroom.

"One of my old friends just came and told me where your father is," she paused, looking up at me, "He is in prison, Eleny."

I gasped, looked down, and covered my face, tears of joy streamed down, I knew that my father was alive, but also tears of great grief, for he was in prison. Everyone searched and searched for my father. It had been seven years since I had seen him.

I'd been little, but I did remember his hands, rough and gentle. His hugs, warm and safe. I missed his kind voice most of all, he would read fairy tales to me, tales of daring knights, stolen princesses, evil kings. But my favorite stories to listen to were the adventures he had as a boy. Enormous fish that pulled him over the boat, wild animals he encountered when hunting, enormous storms that lifted up the barn.

I wish that I didn't remember grandmother crying in the night over her lost son, though.

"Why is he in prison?" I gave a muffled cry.

"I do not know, child, but we must keep strong, and pray," grandmother wrapped her arms around me.

When we came back to the living room I sat in a cushioned chair, wiping away my tears. Palana and I eventually fell asleep in the warm room as I watched the fire lights cast shadows on grandmother's face, as she stayed awake.

I was in a dark room, there was a Thasfaen man on the floor in front of me, he was... injured.

Walking up to him, I saw that he looked almost exactly like me, but with short blond hair, instead of long dark brown hair. He had my tan skin, pointed ears, dark amber eyes, and pointed chin. He had laugh lines and a short, scruffy beard.

Crying out, he touched my arm, his hands were rough and calloused. Tears streamed down his face, I started sobbing, knowing I couldn't help him.

"Eleny........ Eleny," he called, as if I were far away. He stopped breathing.

I there stayed that way, sobbing for what seemed like an eternity.

Something gave me a gentle tug, I opened my eyes to see my grandmother in front of me.

"Eleny, it's midnight and time to leave," she said.

I saw the Thasfaen mother gathering items around the room, so I stood and started helping.

"I have an idea," I said, running to my room

and grabbing a long, thick shawl for winter. I brought it back and gave it to the woman. "You can wrap Omar around you with this." She thanked me and went to get the baby.

"I'm not so sure of this," I murmured, biting my lip. I needed to get out of that habit.

Grandmother noticed my tense expression. "It is alright, you do not have to come if you do not want to, I shall be back in the morning if you do decide to stay."

When Palana came back the baby was still asleep, wrapped around his mother on her back.

"I want to do this. I'm just frightened, doing this is illegal and there are soldiers throughout town," I glanced at Grandmother then to Palana and Omar.

Palana gave me a petrified face, "What if they see him on my back?"

So for her comfort I also gave Palana a little cape so it wasn't so obvious.

Thank goodness the baby isn't awake. He would be awfully loud.

When we were ready to leave, I looked out the back entrance.

"It's clear," I whispered.

The cold night air was unwelcoming and I

heard the crickets giving off their eerie music. We sneaked out the back of the cottage. I ducked under the clothes line and held it up for the others then let my grandmother lead.

It's the middle of the night, everyone is asleep so we should be safe, but we still need to be cautious.

We started to walk through the streets, crept in the shadows, and stayed dead silent. There were only a few dim torches to light the streets.

When we reached the edge of town, I heard somebody speak, a soldier came up behind us. *He must be a sentry on watch.*

"What are you doing at this hour? It is past curfew." he barked. The baby woke up, and moaned under the cape.

"What was that?" the soldier demanded.

Since we were in the dark, he couldn't see the lump on the Thasfaen woman's back. We ignored the man and kept walking, now faster.

The baby started wailing louder, then Palana cried out, "Help!"

Grandmother and I went to see what was wrong, she cried out again, the baby kept wailing.

I lifted the cape and gasped, we saw that the baby had grabbed on to his mother's skin, and was pulling at it. Horrified, we went into the light and I got him out of the wrap, but then the soldier saw what the baby did and sounded the alarm.

Great! Just Great! I took off running into the forest as fast as I could. We had to dodge branches and jump over roots, it was a thick forest and I faltered many times.

Men behind me shouted as I followed grandmother, holding the child tighter. She stopped.

I glanced up and saw the silhouette of a mountain range against a starlit sky.

We had reached the Wall.

There were men still shouting behind us, I took notice of glowing torches not far away. We ran to the Wall, grandmother stopped at a boulder.

Glancing back, the blood drained from my face. Soldiers came up behind us, there were about ten, there was no way we could win a fight against them.

Grandmother somehow moved the boulder, uncovering a hole.

I handed the baby back to his mother, as my grandmother looked at her.

"Go into the tunnel," then looked at me, "do you remember the way?"

"Yes," I answered shakily.

"Alright, go into the tunnel, go to Jone Samb, a Xelman, in Shepla, he shall care for you." She urged me to the tunnel.

"Wait, are you not coming with me?" I was completely afraid of the answer.

I didn't get one because out of nowhere an arrow sliced through the air, inches away from my face. I looked at Grandmother and gasped yet again. She jumped right in front of me, an arrow pierced her back.

"Grandmother!" I cried as she fell to the ground. I knelt down on my knees next to her. The soldiers were getting closer.

"G-go to Jone, tell him that I sent you," she whispered.

The Thasfaen woman looked out the tunnel, "Come!" she called.

I didn't hear her, all I saw was the woman that had loved me, who was now fading, letting go of life.

We stared at each other, time stopped. But then Palana grabbed my arm and pulled me out of sight, through the dark, scary hole.

TWO

Gone

No, no, no!" I shrieked at the woman.

"Come, it's too late, she is gone," Palana said, moving the big stone that served as a door.

But I don't want her to be gone, I don't want her to be! I want to have her warm arms around me, to help me know what to do next!

I cried and cried, until I drifted into sleep.

When I woke up on the cold, dirty floor of the passage, I groggily peered around. Sunlight was shining through cracks in the wall, where a big stone was.

Where was I?

I found the Thasfaen woman with the child in her arms, looking down at me, "It is time for us to go," she said.

Oh, I'm here. "What time is it?" I asked her.

"I don't know, I can't tell in here, most likely around first light," she replied softly.

I stood up and brushed off my brown dress. We ate, then gathered our things.

"I think I remember the way," I said to the woman, she nodded. I surveyed the tight cave and started staggering into the tunnels, leaning on the walls to keep steady.

Left, right, straight, then walk on the road all the way to Shepla. The tunnel shifted, and I saw, with the little light we had, that it turned left. Eventually, I couldn't see a thing.

"Did we bring torches?" I squinted.

"Yes, I shall get one," she answered. I heard a ruffled noise then I saw Palana's face with a torch in one hand and the baby in the other. I took the torch from her and looked around.

"How did you light it?" I wondered.

"Your grandmother brought flint in the sack

she packed," she explained.

"Oh. C-can I have the sack?"

She passed it to me.

I squeezed it to my chest, it was the last thing I had of hers. The faint smell of roses drifted up to my nose. This must have been the bag she would put the roses in when she picked them.

There were two tunnels up ahead, I went to the one on the right, I had already turned left before.

"Okay, we just need to go straight now," I said.

We kept walking, and walking, and walking.

When are we going to get out of here? Did I take a wrong turn? Just as the thought crossed my mind, I saw a faint light up ahead. I glanced back and saw the Thasfaen. She wore a solemn expression and dust covered her face, but she kept the sleeping baby under the cape.

"I see light!" I whisper-shouted.

Immediately she smiled.

I picked up a faster pace and as the cool wall of the tunnel made my hands shiver. We kept getting closer and closer to the light. When I went through the exit it took a moment for my eyes to adjust to the lighting.

Before me was the most stunning forest I had ever seen. The oak trees in Patera were gnarled and twisted, these were tall with leaves that looked like sewing needles. The fragrance of the flowers smelled as sweet as the pies my grandmother used to bake. The bugs were buzzing, and the breeze whisked through the green leaves of the trees.

I glanced at the woman and Omar groaned and woke up, so she uncovered him and let him crawl in the cool grass.

Sitting down on a log, I covered my face, everything flashing back to me. I wished my grandmother was there with me.

"She is gone," I wailed, "I didn't even get to say goodbye!" tears streamed from my eyes.

The woman came, embraced me, and ran her fingers through my long hair. I watched the playful little boy pick the pink flowers.

After a minute the Thasfaen got up and looked through her sack. "We shall eat, then go on," she handed me some bread and cheese.

We ate then started heading toward Shepla.

A while later we came upon a road and traveled for a few hours. When we stopped for lunch and went off the road a bit, Palana and the child napped while I kept watch. It was getting cool under the trees Palana called pine.

    I started dozing off when I heard a noise, making me jump up and peer around. The sound of horses came from up the road and I watched through the bushes. A wagon came around a corner with a Thasfaen with the reins in his hands and a little boy was sitting next to him.

    They both had bright smiles on their faces and were talking. It seemed that they were going the same way as we were.

    I stepped out of the bushes to meet them, "Hello, are you on your way to Shepla?" I hollered.

    He saw me, "Do you need a ride?" he whipped the reins and strode up beside me.

    "Yes, but I have someone traveling with me, could you wait for me to get her?"

    Nodding he said, "I have plenty of room in the back of the wagon, you can ride there."

    I ran to get Palana. She was awake, her eyes scrunched together sleepily. When she caught sight of me I told her that we have a ride, we didn't have to walk.

    She stood up, and picked up the baby, who was still asleep. We went to the wagon and got in the back, thanking the Thasfaens. When we were ready the man whipped the reins and we were off.

It took the entire day to reach Shepla, the road was bumpy and the the smell of horses blew by us, but the baby was asleep almost the whole time.

When Omar was awake the boy played with him, giggling whenever the baby made a noise. By the time we made it to the town, the sky was dark and my legs hurt from being cramped in the wagon for too long.

Palana rented a room at an inn and we stayed there for the night. In the morning Palana and her baby departed tearfully.

"I have some family in Meent, a town in The Plains," she sniffed, "Thank you very much, Eleny, I'm sorry about your grandmother, if you are ever in need of help, you are always welcome to come and stay with me."

"I'm grateful that we met, Palana, but I first will follow my grandmother's wishes. Someday we shall meet again," I said, giving her a hug, holding back tears myself.

"Elyon be with you," she called, walking away.

I didn't know what the phrase meant, but I knew it had to be good.

She has been so kind to me. Will *we ever see each other again?* I watched them ride off in a traveler's wagon.

When I came back into the inn from waving them off on the road, I went to the room.

Should I go back to Polos? No. They saw my face, if I went back they would probably put me in prison.

I packed up my things in the rose sack and inched down the creaky stairs. When I came to the entrance the innkeeper was at the counter.

"Do you know where Jone Samb, the Xelman is?" I asked, licking my chapped lips. It was dryer here than in Patera.

The Thasfaen man looked at me with either a disgusted or confused face, I couldn't tell. "I know where he is, he's crazy! So for your safety, I ain't telling you," his eyebrows pushed together.

"Please, I need to know," I told him calmly.

"I say again, I ain't telling you!" his face started to turn red. Seeing how annoyed he was, I knew that his mind was set.

I guess I will have to ask someone else. Turning around, I exited the inn. *And I don't mind one bit.*

When I came to the dusty street, a baker's bread aroma came and filled my nose. I heard the clatter of a salesman shouting and the horses' clip-clop of hooves.

Something caught my eye and I looked down.

A silver coin!

Picking it up, I ran my finger over the smooth metal. I ran across the busy road, to the baker's shop, and picked up some bread.

I smiled. *It's been forever since I got food without being chased!*

I brought it to the counter and asked the baker about Jone.

"Yes, I'll tell you where he lives, but you don't wanna go there, he's crazy. He tries to boggle your mind, filling it up with nonsense." he scowled, "But he lives at the edge of town, down that road on the right, into the forest down a path," he pointed.

I thanked him, took a bite of bread, and started for Jone.

After walking a quarter of the hour, I reached the cottage and observed the little building. It was covered in vines and appeared to be a pale blue color before the vegetation took over. The pine trees around it loomed overhead. I traipsed up to the old, cracked, wooden door and knocked.

A bedraggled voice came through and the door opened. "What do you want?" His eyes got big.

In front of me was a tall, old, Xelman man, with a stringy old beard, jet black hair, gray eyes, and smelled of... apples?

Shaking the thought away, I introduced myself. "I'm Eleny Nil, my grandmother, Fenmy Nil, sent me to you."

"Oh," his eyebrows shot up, "Oh, I do know your grandmother."

"Did know, I'm afraid," I said, looking down.

"Did?" he asked, leading me into what looked like a dining room and asked if I wanted something to eat.

I said yes, so he left and came back with a tray full of ham, rolls, and cheese. He left again and came out with another tray with tea and sweets on it.

Jone said to take what I want. Of course I said thank you, then I filled a plate full of food, I had only a bite since breakfast. After I ate my fill, he asked again what happened.

I began to tell him of the woman and my grandmother. A deep longing for her built up inside me. I started tearing when I told him that my grandmother had died for me.

Out of nowhere I heard a voice speak in my head. *"I know that it was hard for you to tell me that, dear."*

I stared at Jone with large eyes, he nodded. "I can mindvoice, and so can you," he grinned.

I did not.

"I can mindvoice?" I chortled, "Yeah, sure, and there's a magical wizard outside cleaning your windows."

Ha, *Eleny Nil, you just met Jone Samb, a man who really* is *crazy.*

"No I'm not, I'm telling the truth! You just told me that I was crazy."

My mouth dropped open, "You heard me think?" I stood up. *I need to get out of here.*

"No, you told me!"

"And how, exactly?"

"By mindvoicing!" he exclaimed, "But don't worry, I shall teach you how to do it, but in the morning. It is now time for bed, and you have a lot to learn."

I looked out a window, it was already dark. Time flew by so quickly, it was too late to go back to the inn.

He stood abruptly and gestured for me to

follow, I was so dazed I didn't realize I was walking after him. He showed me to a room.

In the room there was a small bed on the right and a window with a table in front of it on the left. I looked out the window at a garden with the sun setting behind it. There were roses, apple trees, bushes full of berries, and a little bird bath with sparrows in it.

"You may live here as long as you want to," Jone said.

"Uh, thank you, sir?" *What am I getting into?*

"Just call me Jone."

"Well then, thank you Jone. I think I am going to rest for a while, if you don't mind," I answered, really meaning that I needed to think about what just happened.

"Of course, of course, you have been on a long journey."

After he left, I rested, watched the birds, and listened to their quarrels. *Should I even stay here? Should I listen to the baker instead? But my grandmother said to come here, and I have nowhere else to go.* I sighed. *I guess I'll just have to trust Grandmother's words.*

Then I went to bed.

When the sun rose my stomach started to growl, I went to the kitchen and found Jone cooking eggs. I sat at the old wood table and waited for him to finish.

When he did, he brought the food to the table and sat down.

"Mm that was delicious," I said after I finished eating, wiping my mouth with a rag. At least he could cook and I got free food.

"Why thank you, dear," He took a sip of hot tea and gulped, "now, I think it is time to get down to business."

"I guess."

He continued, "Now, just to make sure you can mindvoice, do you sense when a person is coming near you?"

Puzzled, I answered a slow, "Yes."

"Do you feel someone's emotions?"

"Actually," I squeezed my rag, "yes!

"Let us start, so when you want to talk to someone, you first ask permission by telling them your name. If they say 'Welcome' then you can talk to them, if they say, 'Busy' or 'Go' then they either can't or won't talk to you. Now, to protect yourself, you need to say 'Elyon imi kudoz'."

"Okay now I *know* you're crazy."

He rubbed his brow and sighed, "'Elyon imi kudoz' is 'Elyon is with me' in the Old Ones' language, I'm not crazy."

"Fine, you're not crazy. But Elyon? Who's Elyon?"

"Who is Elyon? You can't be serious! Elyon is the One who created life, who created me, who created everything! He is my, and your, heavenly Father!" Jone proclaimed, raising his hands, "and He made you with mindvoicing abilities."

I looked at him like he was crazy. Then I started remembering, my grandmother *did* talk about a creator every now and then, I just didn't pay attention. Then I remembered what Palana said to me when she left. I looked back at him.

"I know who he is, my grandmother spoke of Him."

"Good, do you follow Him?" he asked.

"Um, I think I should want to know more about Him first, if I decide to at all," I snorted.

We walked outside into the gardens and talked late into the afternoon.

He said that Elyon loved me.

It was kind of hard to believe, after all I'd done.

Many people said that their gods loved

them.

Jone also said that there was a book, Elyon's Word, full of His wisdom and laws that we needed to follow. I asked if he had a copy of the book, he said no.

Of course he doesn't.

He knew a woman who did, but she lived up in the mountains. When we stopped talking, without a thought of food or drink, I withdrew to my room and fell fast asleep in the soft blankets of my bed, grandmother's rose bag clutched in my arms, exhausted from the long day.

THREE

Finding The Way

My heart was thumping loudly in my chest. Sweat coated my forehead and neck. I was in a dark forest, dark creatures surrounded me, getting closer and closer. They were ugly and inside of them there was something dark. A void.

One snarled and jumped to attack me and I tried to scream, but nothing came.

Then a bright force appeared, I had to close my eyes, it was so bright that my eyelids lit up. I heard roars, then everything went quiet as they all ran off. A warmth enveloped me and I knew that I was safe.

Still not able to open my eyes, I heard a voice, "Eleny, do not be afraid, I will protect you and be with you all the way," it said, "I am Elyon, and I want you to follow me, you were always meant to." It was loud, but gentle and kind, then it disappeared, taking the light but leaving the warmth for the rest of the night.

In the morning I took a warm bath, put my dress back on, and ate some eggs that Jone had cooked.

"Jone, sir?"

He turned his head up from his plate and latched on to my gaze, "Yes?"

"I feel like you should hear what happened to me last night. . ." I told him what had happened to me in the dream.

He was silent for a few minutes, then finally spoke. "If what you say is true, I believe something evil was trying to attack you last night, and not just evil, but Deceiver," he flipped the egg, "then Elyon saved you from a horrible night, full of nightmares and pain. The reason the evil had attacked you, I think, was because Elyon needs you. Deceiver and his followers want to discourage you and much more."

I stared at him for another five minutes at least. *He's right.*

"I want to follow Elyon, He wanted me to. When He spoke it was— it was like a warmth I've never felt enveloped me," I looked down and smiled, "And Grandmother! I am very sure that she believed in Elyon, she was joyful almost all the time, even during the hardships! She was so kind and helped the needy so much, giving so much away! I really want that joy!"

"Yes, she was raised to know Elyon and knew that He was also her heavenly Father. But are you sure that you want to follow Him, that you would always try to obey His Word?"

"Yes," I said, looking back up, "I do. I just need some help to understand some of it."

"Then you need to give your heart to Him."

"Give your heart to— how? Most other people give their gods offerings."

He frowned and shook his head, "Elyon does not want earthly possessions, for there is no use for them where He lives. Ask Him to forgive your mistakes and ask for Him to come into your heart."

"That simple?"

"That's it, just talk to Elyon, 'Commit your way to Him, trust in Him, and He shall bring forth your righteousness as a light,' that is in Elyon's Word."

"Um," I was as nervous as I could get.

Jone must have noticed after another moment of silence, "Just speak your heart to Him, don't be shy."

I closed my eyes, wondering if that was the right thing to do. "Um, Elyon, I'm not very sure what to say or do, but I want to commit my life to You and trust You, show me what is Your way, what You want me to do. Please forgive me of what I have done in the past, help me to learn what is right. Not only right, but what You want. Please come into my heart, I am Your, um, humble servant."

Before I knew it, unexpected tears were streaming down my face from the shining, warmth that was inside of me. Why was I crying from this feeling? I knew why. It was a love I'd never experienced.

I opened my eyes, Jone was also shedding tears. He wiped them. "Welcome to Elyon's Family!" he smiled, "How do you feel?"

"I've never felt this—this feeling. It's the best I have ever felt." We laughed and Jone went to get some kind of sweet candy.

"It is a time to celebrate, for someone has come into Elyon's Family!" he exclaimed.

I smiled, for I did not have a family now, only my father, who is in prison. Mother was gone, and grandmother, who had been my only relative, was gone, too. "Is this what always happens when people come to Elyon?"

"Well, not always, but I get a little excited when someone new joins Elyon's Family."

When Jone finished his desert, he glanced back up at me, "Well then, let us get back to training, do you remember how to protect yourself?"

"Yes," I nodded, twirling my hair through my fingers, "don't I need to say 'Elyon is with me'?"

"In the Old Ones' language. Here, repeat after me. Elyon imi kuzon."

"Elyon...imi...kuzon?"

"Say it again."

"It again."

He laughed.

Then I said it, "Elyon imi kuzon." My arms

were then covered in goose bumps.

"Good, Good, Elyon will always protect you, and if something happens, it is His plan for you. Now, to look into someone's mind you only have to see their face in your mind and say 'mind sight'. Remember, you need to protect yourself when you do this if the person is evil. Do not look into a friend's mind, only do it if it's greatly important, otherwise it is awfully rude to read their thoughts. You could hurt their feelings greatly."

I nodded.

So the rest of the day, Jone taught me how to mindvoice better and taught me more about Elyon, the old man gained more and more of my trust.

"Jone, this is the first time I have been out of Patera, I don't know about hardly anything out here. The only races that I *have* seen are the Thasfaen, because I am one, and few Jinde in Patera. You are the first Xelman I have ever seen. I don't even know what a Minneckin IS!" I told him after dinner.

We ate fish from Waterway, a city in the middle of a lake nearby, for dinner and were now sitting in the living room.

He thought for a moment, "You know the

Thasfaen, most live in Patera, only some live in The Plains. The tan skin tone, small pointy ears, dark eyes, either sapphire blue, dark amber, the green of an olive, and even sometimes midnight black. They do not normally grow higher than five feet tall, unless it is a halflin, who is a mix between two peoples."

"Yes, yes, I already know about them." I said.

He took a big breath, "The Jinde live in The Plains realm, only a few live in the realm of Patera, they are seven to eight feet tall, but even with their height, most are gentle people. The Xelman people live in Shadow Forest, but you will see one every now and then around it, like me."

He continued telling me about the people in the surrounding lands. The Xelman men had black hair, and women had white, they all had pale skin and were very agile, growing from six to seven feet tall. Their eyes are light colors, like the blue hue of a clear river, silver like the clouds on a sunny day, the color of sand on a beach, light sea green, and sometimes even white. Many could mindvoice.

He finally told me about the Minneckins, they were up to two feet tall, were any pale color of the rainbow, and that they glowed bio luminescent. Not many could mindvoice, but they were very merry and almost child like. Most of them live in the Minnek Realm.

"There's also the wix," he smiled and sighed, "They are the most beautiful creatures you will ever see, they are birds that turn into magnificent animals, with the head of a bird and the body of a fox, but I think with longer legs. Their tails are thick, pure muscle, with shimmering feathers. They have enormous wings with long silky plumage. When in wix form they are the size of a large horse. They can be any kind of bird that flies, eagles, sparrows, black birds, and so on. When they are in the form of a wix, they're the same color as their bird form."

I tried to see the amazing creature in my mind.

"But there are also evil creatures," his face grew grim, "they are called Mordens. The despicable things have fur all over them, but walk like a man and have fangs and claws. With beady eyes and large mouths, they have enormous noses. With that they can track and smell things miles away. They are the most ferocious things."

As he told me all these things I shuddered,

remembering my dream, "Jone, how do you know all of this?"

The corners of his mouth turned up, "I used to have a wix bonded to me for many years and we lived in a small village clearing in Shadow Forest. There were Mordens all throughout the hunting grounds, and I fought them to protect the others that were with me when we hunted."

He had a wix? Wixes were illegal in Patera, but not in the other parts of Iyim.

"I didn't know that you could have a wix," I said curiously, making it obvious I wanted to hear more.

"You can't, they bond to you, you do not own them, they just stay with you for the rest of his or your life as a friend," he stated.

"What happened to yours?"

He stared at the flames in the fireplace, distant. "One night when we went hunting, just Linton and I, that was his name, we got ambushed by at least twenty Mordens. One struck one of Linton's wings before he could take off into the air with me on his back. Linton tried to fly, but with one wing damaged, he could not get off the ground. I tried to protect him, but there were too many. There was pain in the back of my head, then all went dark, and I woke up to a lifeless wix beside me." The old Xelman looked solemnly away.

"I am sorry Jone, I didn't mean to bring back such memories," I mumbled.

His mouth turned into a loving smile again, "He was an amazing creature, strong but gentle, hard-headed but intelligent, and most of all, a wonderful friend. His bird form was a red tailed hawk, he was a very fast flier, and of course his tail was red. He was a reddish brown and speckled white with a pale yellow chest. His wings were magnificently colored with browns, tans, and yellows." Jone gazed into the fire as if Linton were right in front of him. We stayed there for a while until Jone fell asleep in the cozy room on the large cushioned chair.

I then slipped into my warm bedroom and went to sleep.

I tip-toed to the kitchen and found Jone making an omelet. He glanced up at me, looked back at the omelet, then looked back up and stared at me, eyebrows pushed together.

"What?" I asked, puzzled.

"Are those the same garments you wore yesterday?" he asked.

I looked at my tan dress and worn shoes, "Um... yeah." I looked back at him and shrugged, "I didn't bring any more. We were in a hurry."

"Well then, I shall get some more clothing for you, we'll go to town after lunch," said Jone, as he flipped the omelet.

After we ate I practiced mindvoicing to Jone, and tried to look into his mind. After a few hours of practicing, we ate lunch, a pork sandwich with tomatoes and lettuce from his garden.

When we were done, we walked to town. There were shops, an inn, and a tavern.

He put money in my hand, "You can use this to get your garments, I have never been good at shopping for women, so you can get what you like," he smiled.

"Thank you so much, Jone," I said, wondering why he was doing all this for me.

"I shall be in the tavern," then he added quietly, "If you need me just mindvoice to me."

I glanced down at the coins in my hand. I hadn't had new clothes in a long time.

When I first went to the dress shop, I bought a plain dark blue dress with black trim, a gray dress, and a black cape with a hood. Next I went to a tailor's, for they were the only place that held them, and got black boots and a pair of simple gray shoes, I bought nothing that was too expensive so there was a lot left over. I brought them up to a young Thasfaen woman, with a baby girl on her hip, at a counter.

"You're not from around here, are you?" the young woman said, eyeballing me.

"No, I'm not," I answered sweetly, smiling at the little one. She was adorable. Her thin, wispy, blonde, hair was flowing down to her shoulders. Freckles covered her face.

I gave the woman the money and she wrapped the shoes in paper. I said goodbye then left the store. When I was done I told Jone.

Eleny Nil to Jone Samb.
"Welcome"
I'm done, are you still at the tavern?
"Yes, I will meet you at the entrance," he answered.

I started walking over to the tavern. He walked out and I ran to meet him in the street. There were wagons and people on the busy roads of Shepla, I had to dodge many of them. Most of them were Thasfaens, but I did see a Xelman or Jinde every once in a while. I finally reached the Xelman and started walking with him back to his little house.

"Jone Samb to Eleny Nil."

Welcome

"I just heard that there are raids going on in towns across Iyim."

Raids?

"Yes, nobody knows who is behind them, but they say they are vicious."

I prayed for Elyon to help the people that had lost family members, and wondered if He heard me.

When we started walking back to the Jone's cottage, an evil presence lurked, I looked at Jone, and he seemed worried, he felt it too. We passed the inn, the feeling was getting heavier.

I gasped, out of nowhere men in black stormed into the town on horses with clubs and swords. One rode up to a young man and clubbed him, while another threatened a woman who was screaming. I smelled smoke. Following my nose I found that a house was on fire.

"Water! We need water!" I heard men shouting.

"I have to help!" I told Jone, quickly running to the voices.

The women of the town made a chain of

people with buckets of water, while the men took up anything they could find and fought the men in black. They had a disadvantage, the men in black had powerful horses. I ran to help the women.

When the fire was out I walked up to Jone sweating.

"Well done, Eleny. I would not be able to pass many buckets at my age," he said, patting my shoulder.

I gave a weak smile and rubbed my head, an ache was forming at the back. *Probably from the ashes and noise.*

I looked around, the men in black were gone, but the terrified people's feelings still lingered. When everyone started to clean up, I heard a woman wailing, it was the one that was at the dress shop. Others were around her saying comforting words.

"They took my child! My little girl, they took her!" she sobbed.

"Why would they take an innocent infant?" I asked Jone when I went back to him.

"I do not know, let us go back to my cottage and see if they did anything to it."

When we stepped on to the path that led to the cottage, I felt another evil presence. Right before I took another step, a tall, beefy man in black walked out of the thick forest and stood in front of us.

Elyon imi kuzon. Oh Elyon please help us.

"Aaargh!" He ran up to us with a club and tried to attack us, so we started to run.

I went into the bushes off the path, "Jone, hurry!" I said, lips trembling.

Suddenly Jone tripped and fell, "Don't come out whatever happens!" he told me.

I watched the man come up behind him. I closed my eyes, for I couldn't watch. I heard the man beat him, after he finally left I ran to Jone. He was badly wounded and unconscious.

"Oh n-no, Jone!" I cried. I looked down at his bruised, wrinkly face, his clothes were covered in blood and dirt.

I knelt down, hot tears ran down my face. *Why would something happen like this? He was a good man! Why Elyon?*

Then, all of a sudden, a sense of peace came in my heart, somehow I knew everything would be alright. Warmth flowed through me, into Jone. But something, or someone, else was with me, that was giving the warming peace.

Elyon imi kuzon.

My hands started glowing on Jone's chest, first my finger tips, knuckles, then my to my palm. His dark bruises turned red, then pink, then to his normal pale skin tone. His breathing increased. After a few more minutes my hands dimmed, the light faded.

Jone shifted, then sat up, without bruises and wounds, healthy! He looked up at me with wide eyes and a smile.

I hugged the old man and kissed his cheek. "What happened?" I cried shakily, "I thought you were dead!"

"I don't quite know, let's get back to the cottage," Jone told me.

We walked silently all the way to the little house, then sat at the kitchen table. By the time I sat down I was exhausted, about to pass out.

"I think that you have powers," Jone sat.

"Powers? Did mindvoicing do it?" I yawned.

He shook his head, "No. Your father went to prison for a reason, I think that reason is because he was trying to protect you from being killed. To keep you alive he gave you to your grandmother to go into hiding. In Polos no one knew you or your grandmother, so you were safe. Either Fenmy knew you had powers, and did not tell you for your own safety, or your father did not tell her."

I thought for a minute, "What powers do you think I have?" I asked.

"I think you have some kind of healing powers," he answered, "Do you remember the woman I told you about, the one with a copy of Elyon's Word?"

"Yes, she lives up in the mountains, who is she?"

"She is another Xelman, her name is Raeya Pinsa, she has powers of her own, and knows more about Elyon," he said, "You need to go to her, I have taught you all I can."

After we were done talking I staggered to my room and stared out to the garden to think. *I can't believe I have powers! But now I need even more training. What happens after that? I don't know.* I gazed at all of the life in the garden, the fruits and flowers, the birds in the trees, everything was so peaceful.

I thought there was more to these raids. A dark feeling entered inside of me whenever I thought about it. Something was going on that no one knew about, and it was likely bigger than just

a raid like this one.
    Thinking about this, I collapsed on my bed.

FOUR

Preparations

In the morning Jone was standing over the table. On the table was a well-worn map of Iyim. He pointed at a dotted line.

"Do you know how to use a compass and map?"

I shook my head, yawning.

"Well, you are going to need them when you travel, so let's start."

The rest of the day I learned how to use the tools and packed for my trip.

I was about to go to bed, I had packed my clothes, including my old ones, the map and compass that Jone had given me, and a blanket, in grandmother's rose sack. I was leaving in the morning.

"Jone, how long will it take for me to get there?" I asked in my door way, about to go to bed.

"Well my dear, that depends, but I would think about three days by foot." he answered.

Three days…by myself…and on foot…

"Why can't you come with me? Don't you want to see Raeya again?" I asked eagerly, biting my lip.

"No I cannot come with you, I am too old." he smiled sadly, "Traveling does not suit me well. But I shall check on you by mindvoicing every now and then. Also, if you need any help, just ask permission, and if I do not answer, I am either asleep or dead!" he said laughing.

I didn't laugh.

"I shall tell Raeya when you leave and that you are coming so she shall know." he told me.

Thank goodness, I wouldn't want to come without her knowing.

We said goodnight and I tried to go to

sleep. Unfortunately I couldn't fall asleep so I got out of bed, walked quietly to the back door, and stepped into the garden. It was my favorite place to be and it was where I was when I wasn't training or helping around the house.

I stepped into the cool grass with bare feet and sat down on a bench. It was a clear night, the moon was out, and the breeze was cool. I heard the crickets and smelled the apples that were covered by darkness.

Apparently the reason Jone smelled like apples when I first knocked on his door was because he had just come inside from picking them.

It'd been a week since I'd came to Shepla.

I looked around and thought of my grandmother and how she would love this place. We had had a garden, full of zinnia, phlox, and tulips, but it wasn't as large as this.

I wonder if Grandmother could mindvoice? Isn't mindvoicing hereditary? Maybe my mother or father had the ability.

"Can't sleep?" said a voice.

My heart pounded as I looked and behind me was Jone with a lantern.

"Jone, you nearly made me jump out of my

socks!" I put my hand on my heart.

He gave a chuckle, "Sorry, dear."

"And no," I said, pulling my knees up to my chin, "I guess I'm a little nervous about tomorrow."

"Just like your grandmother." he looked up at me and grinned, "She couldn't sleep even if she was only going to a nearby town."

"Really?" I asked.

"When we were children we lived in the same town, and our fathers and mothers traded goods. Like grain, livestock, eggs, and anything that the other needed at the time," he answered. My eyes started to droop while listening to Jone's calming voice. He told me adventures of him and Grandmother for a while until I yawned again.

"Jone, thank you for telling me all of those things. Grandmother never spoke much about when she was a little girl. I'm going to turn in for the night, I have a long few days ahead of me, see you in the morning," I said, yawning again.

"Good night, dear," I heard him say behind me.

I went to the back door, through the hallway, and stepped into my room. Right when my head touched the pillow my eyes closed and I fell asleep thinking of Grandmother's childhood.

Opening my eyes, I took a deep breath, smelling apples in the garden. I got dressed in my new gray dress, black boots—I had thrown my old shoes away— for the trip. Jone gave me a pack. When I put all of my belongings in the pack I would be ready to leave after I ate breakfast.

Jone had baked a special cake. It was full of apples and blueberries. He called it the double fruit pie, as long as it had two fruits or berries in it, that was what it was called.

I went to the table and sat down in front of him then sliced a piece. "Good morning, Jone, this is a nice surprise," I said, taking a bite of the warm, fruity flavor, "Mm, this is a delicious cake! Thank you."

"Good morning, my mother had always baked this for me when I was going on a journey, and I thought you would enjoy it," he served himself a piece, "Well, if you leave soon you should get there the day after tomorrow."

I stopped eating and looked at him, "But I am going to be all alone!" I frowned, "I'm only sixteen, I'm only four feet tall, and there are not-so good people on the road, and wild animals on the mountains for that matter."

"You are not alone, Elyon is always with you and he will protect you." He gazed at me with his warm, light, gray eyes, "talk to Him, it has always helped me to say 'Elyon is with me' when I am afraid. It also protects you from people peering into your mind, the fear could even be from someone putting thoughts in your head."

"People can put thoughts in my head?" I squeaked, eyes getting big.

"Raeya can tell you about it when you get there, if I start telling you now then half the day would be over when I finish."

"Oh, well I need to go now before it gets any later in the day, the sun is almost at its peak," I sighed. Standing up, I picked up my pack and started for the door, but first I turned around and ran to the old Xelman and gave him a hug and gave him a kiss on his wrinkled cheek, "Thank you for everything that you have done for me, shall I *ever* see you again?"

"My dear, if we do not see one another again here in this world, we shall see each other in Elyon's House."

I nodded and stepped up to the door. When I reached it I turned around to take one last look at the Xelman, trying to etch the picture into my mind so I would never forget his face. He followed me but stopped at the door.

Tears welled in my eyes, this man had helped me so much. "Good bye, Jone."

"Good bye, Eleny dear, Elyon be with you,"

When I reached the end of the path I looked back again and saw the little house, covered in vines and little flowers climbing the walls, with Jone in the doorway. I turned back around and started on my journey.

I kept walking and walking down the road. The scenery was beautiful, pine trees were on both sides of me. The birds were tweeting in the branches.

When I stopped to have lunch and rest for a moment I looked at the map. There was supposed to be a river that fed into the lake Waterway was over.

After I finished eating my lunch of bread and an apple on the green grass, I continued my journey.

When the sun started getting low, my feet started to hurt from the long walk. I heard the sound of rushing water. Picking up my pace, I eventually saw the river, it was at least a hundred yards wide.

How am I going to cross it? It is so wide, and it looks like it's deep, too. I might have to swim, didn't Jone think of this? Oh right, he had probably either a wix or some friends last time he was even on this road.

I rolled my eyes at the thought and sighed. The sun was setting behind the trees now, and the breeze was getting colder. I turned back and went into the woods a little ways. Taking the rose sack off my shoulder, I grabbed the blanket inside, I then brought out a match and made a fire out of the sticks around me. I laid the blanket out on the cold ground and sat down, then pulled out some food for dinner. When I was finished eating I snuggled up under the blanket next to the warmth of the flames.

But right when my eyes started to close, I heard a screech pierce the air. I jumped up, gasping, and looked around. Another screech made my heart race as fast as the river nearby. Since it was dark I couldn't see but a few feet from the fire. I picked up a stick and set it a glow.

Elyon imi kuzon. Elyon is with me.

The warmth enveloped me, the same feeling when Elyon came to me in the dream and when I healed Jone. I peered around and saw something small move in the bushes. I stepped a bit closer, pushing a branch away, then looked down and saw a ball of feathers and fluff. It was some kind of bird, it turned around, eyes closed. It had a heart shaped face that was pure white with a few scuffles of dirt around the edges. Its wings were a buff color, its breast was a soft white. Its size was the length from my elbow to my wrist, which was pretty small compared to my height.

I picked up the creature, it appeared injured, one of its wings were twisted the wrong way. I brought it to my blanket and looked closer.

I closed my eyes and put my hands on the soft feathers to heal it like I did Jone. I thought 'Elyon is with me' when I did it to him, so I did it again.

Elyon imi kuzon.

The familiar peace came over and my hands lit up again, as if fire was underneath. The wing twisted back into place and the wounds sealed up. When I lifted my hands to see, the bird was completely healed.

I did it, I healed it! Thank you Elyon.

It wasn't conscious so I covered it up in my blanket and went into an exhausted sleep.

I heard a high-pitched voice.

"*Me can't breath!*" it screamed. I sat up and looked around, heart pounding. The sky was gray with some birds flying above the trees. I glanced down and where I covered up the bird the little lump was moving. I lifted the blanket and looked at the creature. It peered up at me and gave a little hiss, but then it gave somewhat of a smile and the voice in my head spoke again.

"*Why me healed?*"

Are you the one who is mindvoicing me?

"*Yes.*" At the same time the animal nodded, her voice was hooty, but also elegant.

Birds can mindvoice?

"*No, birds no mindvoice,*" the creature answered, tilting her head as if confused.

But you are *a bird.*

"*No me am a* WIX."

A wix?

"*Yes, wix.*"

FIVE

A New Bond

I stared at the heart-shaped face creature, dumbfounded.

So you can shape-shift? I mindvoiced.

She stood up and answered, "*Yep,*" she then gazed into my eyes.

It was as though she saw into my soul, it was a very strange feeling.

"What's your name and what're you?"

My name is Eleny Nil. I'm a Thasfaen.

"*Me now bonded to you, Eleny Nil, now me go where you go, me help where me can, and me be your life friend!*" she said happily.

What's your name?

"Noctua," she said, *"and me bird form is barn owl, so me am a barn owl wix."*

How were you wounded if you could turn into a wix?

"A opossum, one of barn owl's biggest enemies, attack me before me could transform," she wilted, *"apparently it was his tree me was perched on. me fell from the tree and landed in the bushes."* Noctua glanced back up at me, "Hmm, me heard you talking about crossing river, in morning me shall turn into wix and you ride on me."

Huh.

At that I got under my covers and watched Noctua snuggle in the blankets near my feet. I decided to figure out what had just happened in the morning, so I closed my eyes and dozed off.

I was soaked with dew, and so was the blanket, when I awoke. The fire was out. I uncovered, stood up and stretched.

Where's, oh what was her name again—Noctua? I bit my lip and gazed around at the trees. *Yes, Noctua, did she leave?*

Suddenly something grabbed me, I jumped and looked up, Noctua was on my shoulder.

Eleny Nil to Noctua.

"No need do that, you thoughts pop up in my head, and not many people can block their wixes. When you want to get my attention just call me by me name."

Oh, I didn't know. So I can't block you from reading my mind?

She whistled, *"No."*

How did I not hear you coming?

"Barn owls are very silent fliers in the owl species. Also they have most best hearing out of all owl kind!"

I could tell she liked to talk about herself. Her chest puffed out, her feathers puffed up, and she lifted her head high. I smiled as she flew off my shoulder and flapped her buff-colored wings, hovering in front of me.

"Pack your things, me change when you ready."

When I put my blanket in my rose sack I watched Noctua, who was perched on a branch on a tree nearby.

I'm ready, Noctua.

"Then is time for me to turn into wix."

All of a sudden, a soft golden light swirled around the barn owl as she came and landed on the ground, when the light faded a stunning creature replaced it. She had the head of a bird, the body of a fox, and poofy tail. Her paws looked soft, but no claws showed. Two round, pale orange-pink horns looked like a crown upon her head. Her beak was a light orange-pink, too. She had the same colors that she had before, her face was white as snow, her chest was light cream, her tail was the buff color with gray spots. She was as tall as a horse, but much more majestic, in my opinion. She was amazing. She unfolded her wings, they were enormous, golden and glistening with gray spots on top, and on the inside they were the soft, pure white.

     She walked up and ducked her head for me to reach. I gently smoothed down the ruffled feathers on her head, she relaxed when I did this. Closing her eyes she gave a little whistle.

"Get on my back, and we fly across river." Noctua opened her eyes and jumped up, she excitedly turned and gestured for me to get up.

     I jumped and tried to get my leg over her back, but failed.   Noctua's big golden eyes focused on me. She made a funny noise with her throat. It almost sounded as if she was laughing at me.   I grimaced, then tried and failed again. Frustrated, this time I backed up a ways and ran to jump, but it knocked the wind out of me when I hit her and I just ended up on my back on the ground.

Getting up, I sighed and frowned.

I can't get up, I'm too short.

When she laid down and tucked her wings in I knew, right then and there, that if I ever had another wix in my life, she would be the best out of them all. I sat on her back between her neck and wings, on her shoulders. My hands stroked her fur beneath me and I beamed, it was as soft as velvet.

Thanks, Noctua.

"You welcome."

She stood up, spread her wings, and started flapping.

I closed my eyes as the air swirled around me. When I opened them the trees were below us. I grabbed onto Noctua's horns and held on, not wanting to fall.

Elyon imi kuzon, Elyon imi kuzon. The warmth came over.

"You won't fall and if wind knocks you off I catch you."

Good to know.

I sat up and stroked her long feathers. Looking out I could see for miles, I could see Shepla, The Wall, and even the Shadow Forest realm. I took the map out of my pack and surveyed it, trying to keep it from flapping. Near Shadow forest there was supposed to be a mountain range with one larger peak. I peered at the scenery and found it then pointed it out to Noctua.

"*Head to the largest peak in that range.*" I implored, the wind was blowing hard up this high, so I was glad that I didn't have to yell.

About half an hour later I finished telling Noctua where we were going and why, and how I healed her. I didn't exactly tell her, I thought of what happened and she listened. We landed at the bottom of the mountain. I jumped down and looked at the map.

It looks like we can't fly, Noctua, we wouldn't see the place we're going to.

"*Well, me shall turn back into me bird form and fly through trees while you walk.*"

I gawked at Noctua as she transformed back into an owl, the swirling light was soft and feathery until it dissipated and a flying barn owl replaced the wix.

I don't think I shall ever get used to that.
"*Me hope not.*"

Noctua came and landed on my shoulder to look at the map that I held out. We needed to go down a path that had a giant pine tree with a carving of a Wix on it, Jone told me. I looked around then asked Noctua to get above the trees and look for the largest pine. I sat down and looked at the map, it didn't show exactly where Raeya lived. I saw writing on the back of the map, I flipped it over and read aloud,

> *"Look to the east*
> *On the path of a great pine,*
> *You will find what you seek,*
> *On the mountain, vine.*
>
> *Through a crack in the mountain,*
> *Deep and thin,*
> *You will find what you search for,*
> *All is within."*

I thought and thought while I sat, leaning up against a tree, and waiting for Noctua to come back from looking for the giant pine.

Why would Jone put a riddle on the back of the map? Closing my eyes for a moment I took in the smell of the pine. When I opened them Noctua was flying through the trees and landed in my lap.

"I found the great tree you speak about, it's much taller than rest of trees."

I jumped, not used to a voice pop into my head. *Thank you, Noctua.*

I looked down at her and scratched the feathers between her eyes.

I stood up and Noctua climbed up to my shoulder and flew off, I followed.

I was running when she stopped abruptly. In front of me was the tallest tree I had ever seen. As I approached it, with the crunch of pine cones under my feet, I saw a picture of a wix that was carved into the thick, rough, bark. I knew that it was the right tree. I stepped around the tree and at the back smaller pine trees made a straight line. Beside the trees it looked as if a small animal trail was made.

The reason Noctua didn't see it was because it is covered by bushes. I shall have to go under them. The vines! The poem said vines! The vines are the bushes!

"No wonder." Noctua came and landed on my shoulder gently.

Noctua, you might want to either get in my pack or fly over then find me when I come out.

"Hmm, me will fly and hunt then find you, wix can always find it's bonded by a pull. The same for you people to wixes."

I focused on Noctua and frowned. *Noctua,*

am I not your first bonded?

"No, you are first."

I grinned as she continued.

"Every wix mother and father tell their wixen, a little wix who not yet know their bird form, about having bonded and bond between them. Me took off on me own when me can transform into bird, when me was year old and ready to fly. Is only six months since, but wixes grow very fast, like cats and dogs do, but me do not like comparing them with wixes. In wix years me your age." she said matter-of-factually.

Noctua started to smooth down my hair with her beak.

Noctua, what are you doing?

"Oh," she stopped and averted my gaze, *"we wixes preen other's feathers, which, um, is loving touch to another. Me kind of miss it."*

I lifted my hand and smoothed down the feathers between her eyes with my fingers. She closed her eyes and leaned on my head. She stayed there for a few minutes but then took off and said she would meet up with me later.

I said goodbye and watched her fly off, when I couldn't see her anymore it was like a part of me was gone. Like something was missing. Knowing that I needed to get going, I went into the bushes. It was dark and musky inside and the branches kept snagging my hair and dress as I crawled.

I kept crawling until I saw light and stood up as I came out. When I observed my surroundings there was a little trail up ahead with the mountain on the right and the sky and few trees on the left. I told Noctua that I was out and a pulse pulled at me, she came and landed gracefully on my shoulder, her favorite perch.

Sorry it took so long, it was tight and sticks kept scratching me.

"No worry, me caught vole and had time to eat it, me was about to come find you when you called me."

I pointed to the path. *Shall you scout ahead? Look for a big crack in the mountain and tell me if you find it, I'll follow behind.*

She nodded her white face and took off, flying down the path beside the mountain majestically, while I followed.

The leaves were light green, and the sun shined on me through the tree limbs, but it was chilly being higher up on the peak. The trail stopped abruptly, ending at the wall of the mount. I walked to it and looked behind a boulder a little taller than me, there was a small opening.

Noctua, I think I found the way in!
"Me coming!"
Oh, and change into wix form while you're at it.

A few minutes later she came through the trees and was in wix form.

I need help to move this stone, I think the crack is behind it.

She came up and started to push the boulder, her wings and back legs pumping as she did.

When the crack was big enough I went into the dark tunnel. I saw a flash so I looked behind me and Noctua was a barn owl again. I let her fly ahead of me because she could see better in the dark. I crouched while I walked through the spider infested tunnel, but I eventually had to crawl. When something small hit my face I screeched, knocking it off.

I wonder how Noctua got through here? I bet she had a fun time eating these horrible bugs!

I kept crawling until I heard the screech of a barn owl and Noctua came flying through to me. I noticed that the ceiling was getting higher as I crawled so I stood up and held out my arm as she landed. She said that there was a clearing and a small building, and that she came to tell me straight away. She took off again and I followed her until there was an opening.

When I stepped on the green grass I observed my surroundings. We were in a valley and, as Noctua said, there was a little cottage with flower plants and a little white fence in the front. Near a garden with vegetable plants a well with an old bucket sat and weeds grew up from the brick, trees grew around it all. From where I stood a little path led up to the front door. On the right there was a little shed with chickens and chicks roaming in and out of the little doors, and on the left a small pond with ducks and geese waddling through some reeds.

She must like animals.

"*It is making me hungry.*"

I looked at Noctua, who was on a branch in a young oak tree. *Didn't you just have a snack?*

"*You mean yuck spiders? Bleh. Me don't like how them go down my throat, me like big fat juicy voles and rats, mm.*"

I was talking about the vole you had earlier.

"*Oh, me forget about that.*"

I walked up to the house and stepped up to the front door. The little yellow cottage had brown trim and was clean and well taken care of, unlike

Jone's with overgrown vines. I could tell that a woman was living here, hence the flowers and plants in orderly rows.

I knocked on the front door, no answer. I knocked again, still no answer. I saw a trail that led to the back of the house and followed it.

Some goats were eating grass along the fence surrounding them, a fat one stared at me curiously, munching loudly. A mother rabbit stepped out of a hole with three speckled babies following, but they ran back in when they saw me.

I stepped around the corner and there was a porch shaded by trees with an old woman on a rocking chair, she glanced up at me and smiled.

SIX

Learning

Elyon imi kuzon.

I stepped up to the woman, "Hello, I'm Eleny, Eleny Nil," I said, "Jone Samb sent me to you."

"Oh, I know who you are, I just didn't think that you would get here so quickly. Jone said that you would get here tomorrow," she stood up.

Noctua spoke. *"She's old."*

I agreed. The Xelman woman had white hair, a gentle smile, blue eyes as clear as the sky, and was much taller than me. She had many wrinkles across her face, her hands were frail, and she wore a maroon dress and crisp white apron. She lifted a little black bird in her palm and it flew off, cutting through the air.

"I am Raeya Pinsa, this is Mentha, she is a barn swallow wix," she said, pointing to the little black bird, "and I am guessing that you either have a wix too, or that you can run very fast."

"Uh, yes, I do have a wix, I saved her in the forest next to the Way River, she bonded to me and I flew on her to the top peak, that's why I got here today," I told her, "Her name is Noctua, she's a barn owl wix. She's uh, over there," I pointed.

Noctua came flying from the young oak that she was perched on and landed on my shoulder.

"May I?" Raeya asked, and I shrugged and nodded. She reached out her hand and rubbed the owl's head.

Noctua glanced at me nervously with her big black eyes, she must never had been touched by another person except for me. *"Why she touching me?"* Noctua hopped closer to my head, backing away from Raeya.

Maybe because she has never seen a barn owl before?

"Well me no like, me only like when you touch my feathers." said Noctua, hissing loudly at the woman, Raeya jerked her pale hand back, eyes wide.

"I'm the only one who has touched her before, and she says she would rather keep it that way. Don't worry though, her screech is bigger than her bite," I assure her with a chuckle.

"Will she try to eat any of my animals?" she asked, eyes big.

"I don't think she will, but I shall ask," I looked up at the owl. *Noctua would you eat any of her animals?*

"Only mice in shed, me hear one now."

I told Raeya what Noctua told me, she looked relieved and told me that there were many rodents.

When I told Noctua she took off gracefully and gave a screech.

"Me be back later."

Okay.

"We should go inside now, the sun is going down and I have to finish dinner, we will then talk after we eat, follow me," said the Xelman woman, as she walked to the door. She opened it and I followed.

We walked into a spacious room with a lot

of windows covered by curtains, there were a few cushioned chairs and a sofa on one side and a table with chairs on the other.

A delicious smell came to my nose as we came into the kitchen. A window was over a basin and water pump, and cabinets were over a counter. A broad wood stove was in a corner, its chimney was shooting up through the roof, Raeya opened it and pulled out a pan then set it on the counter.

I went and looked inside it, "Mm, what is it?" I asked, smelling the spicy aroma.

"From where I come from it is called pastato, it is pasta and tomatoes with all kinds of spices baked in the oven, I was making it for you for when you would get here tomorrow. I was going to eat some then put it in spring water that was from deep inside this mountain." Raeya looked out the window, "I keep the food that I want to eat there later, the water keeps it cold so it can last longer." She came over and put some salt and pepper on the dish.

We had dinner in the main room, when we were done we cleaned up and sat on the other side of the room. I chose to sit on the flowery sofa and Raeya sat on a cushioned chair. I then told

Raeya everything that happened with my grandmother, Palana, Jone and how I healed him, and that that was the way I healed Noctua.

"Raeya, Jone said that you have powers of your own, and that you could help me with mine," I asked nervously, still wondering if she would help me.

"Well, first of all, they are not 'powers' they are gifts, Elyon gives them. Did Jone tell you what gift I have?"

I shook my head.

"My gift is that of nature, I reach out to the living thing, that is partly why I have so many animals, because they are all dear friends. How do you use your gift?"

"I touch the person or animal, my hands start glowing, and I feel a certain calmness, or peace. Then when my hands darken, they are healed, I've only done it twice."

"Then you do not know much about it?"

"No," I mumbled, trying to stifle a yawn.

"I have a few books that might help, but I shall show you them tomorrow, its late now and time to sleep," Raeya stood up and I followed her to a room through the kitchen with my bag.

There was a large bed, a table, and a

window that filled the wall with plants in the wide windowsill.

"This is the guest room, but since I don't have many visitors it became a sun room for my plants." She set the candle on the table, "Make yourself at home."

We bid each other good night and Raeya left the candle with me. I changed into a nightgown that Raeya let me borrow and checked on Noctua.

Noctua?

"Yes?"

Are you good for the night or do you want to come in here with me?

"Can I?"

I don't think Raeya would mind, she does have a wix of her own. Come to the window.

I went over to a smaller window near my bed and opened it. Gracefully Noctua came and landed on the sil, she found a perch on one of the plants and I got in bed.

When I was comfy I started thinking. *Noctua, aren't you nocturnal, so you're awake during the night?*

"Yes, but my mother and father wixes not barn owl wix, me became barn owl wix when me not wixen *anymore. Me started to be awake at night when me left. But now me switch my sleep time and me is awake when you awake."*

Huh, that makes sense, goodnight Noctua.
"Goodnight."

I looked and her eyes were closed, then I drifted off into a deep sleep.

I woke up with the sun shining through cracks in the curtains and the smell of something baking came to my nose. I got out of bed and tip-toed over to the plants then pulled the curtains back so they would have sunlight, forgetting that Noctua was on one of the little trees.

There were all kinds of flowers! Purples, yellows, pinks, blues, any kind of color you could think of. Noctua opened her eyes and flew to my shoulder to look at them, too.

"They very pretty, me not see this many kind in a long time."

When have you seen this many before?

"Me was little, but we live near a field of flowers and in new season they bloom."

Sounds pretty.

"It was."

When we were done gazing at the plants I

put my tan dress on, I was going to wash the garments I wore the day before.

When I was ready I walked into the kitchen, with Noctua still on my shoulder, and followed my nose to the stove to look inside. Puffy muffins were being baked, they looked and smelled delicious.

I opened the back door and Mentha was flying in and out from under the trees. I looked around the house then finally found Raeya working in the vegetable garden.

"Good morning," Raeya said smiling, "did you sleep well?"

"Yeah, the bed is quite different from the hard ground. Was it alright for Noctua to sleep in the room with me?" I asked. "What are you doing?" I saw that she was picking something from a plant.

"Just getting some basil, rosemary, and some more herbs that healers work with," she answered, "They might help with your training, and yes, if you have a wix they feel most comfortable sleeping by your side," she put the leaves in her basket and stood up, "Come, breakfast is almost done and I have a lot to do." she walked past me and I followed.

"Me glad me can be with you."

Me too. I smiled at her.

We ate muffins with milk and strawberries in the kitchen. When we were done I followed Raeya outside to help with chores around the house. We fed the chickens and chicks corn, then did the same for the ducks and geese. Raeya told me all of their names and who was whose relative, I'd never heard of anything like that before. All the time Noctua was eagerly eyeing the ducklings and chicks, so I was glad when we moved on.

Next we went to feed the goats some hay, and Raeya told me about them also. It turned out that the fat goat I had seen the day before was pregnant, not fat. Her name was Jane, she had a nutty brown hide with little horns poking out between her floppy ears. The babies ran around the other mothers, they were sweet and curious little creatures, and came up to be fed and pet.

I saw the little rabbit and her speckled babies come out of the hole again and asked Raeya about them. The mother's name was Lucy, she was white with brown spots on her back. Same for her children except with black spots instead of brown. I held out a carrot to them and the bunnies came up to me and ate out of my hand. Raeya looked nervously at me, and I remembered that

Noctua was on my shoulder, looking quite anxiously at the little animals. I assured her that Noctua wouldn't eat them, although I was a bit worried again, so I sent Noctua to go find something to eat in the shed. Raeya relaxed when she took off, then said that the father rabbit, he was black, wasn't around very much and was always in the forest, so the babies didn't have as much protection that they needed.

When we finished Raeya showed me to a small room in the house, shelves full of books lined the walls and there was a window and cushioned chair with a table sitting in a corner. Raeya searched the shelves and started passing books to me. When she was done she looked at me and took half the stack.

"We will see if there is anything in these, and if not we can come back for more," she said.

We went to the living room and set the books on the table. Raeya opened the curtains and light filled the room, I now saw that there were plants in here near the windows, too.

When Raeya gave me a brown book I heard a *tap tap tap*. It got louder, *TAP TAP TAP*. I glanced back at the window, and Noctua was on the window-sill.

"Can me come in?"

I stood and opened it, she lifted and perched on my shoulder.

"What you doing?"

Trying to figure out my gift.

"Look for anything with the healing gift," Raeya said, then took one with a dark red cover and opened it. It took a while but Raeya finally found something, she read aloud,

"To heal you have to find peace and bestow it to the person that you touch, Elyon joins you to make a full circle. Only the very powerful can heal without touch. If you use herbs first and then start the healing process it will not take all of your energy. Although it will take up more time unless you either are ready or know exactly what you need to do." she paused, "That is all, the rest is about the other gifts."

"What *are* all the gifts?" I asked.

"Nature, healing, and protection. Elyon gives all of these. But there are also the gifts that Deceiver gives to men who vow to follow him, these are destruction, taking, and control, but there would be a toll to pay. If you had and used the evil gift long enough you would feel nothing, nothing would be inside of you, and you would only feel anger, hate, and fear, you would belong to Deceiver. The only way to get out of his grasp is to turn to Elyon and ask for his forgiveness, if you don't in time you would eventually die and end up in Deceiver's House instead of Elyon's if you didn't."

I tried to grasp all that Raeya had said. *That reminds me.*

"Of what?" asked Noctua.

"Do you have a copy of Elyon's Book?" I asked. "Jone said that you did and that you could teach me more about Him."

That.

Noctua whistled. *"Oh!"*

"You need to learn about Noctua's abilities, too," Raeya said.

"Why would I need to learn about Noctua's abilities?"

"Ahem, me right here."

"Because they can be helpful and you can know how valuable she is," she elaborated.

"Me like her."

I nodded and glanced at Noctua, who was now sitting up in my lap, gazing over the edge of the table.

"Did you ride here in that dress?" Raeya

asked, looking at my clothes.

I nodded, "Why?"

"How ever did you manage?"

I smiled shyly, "Barely."

"Well, then you need some riding clothes. I shall give you some. I think I have some that someone left."

"Oh, thank you!"

"Don't mention it. But, oh my, oh my," Raeya closed the book, "This is a lot to learn, and teach. Oh, and you will also have to learn about herbs and what they do. You do know how to mindvoice, yes?" Raeya asked.

I asked permission. *Eleny Nil to Raeya Pinsa.*

"Welcome, so you do, at least Jone taught you something." She sighed.

I stifled a laugh. Raeya's mind voice was like her normal voice, calm, but full of fun.

"Alright," Raeya started, *"try to pry into my mind, we are going to practice some mindvoicing first, it is always good to exercise your mind sometimes."*

I cut off the connection I had with Raeya and started to pry into her mind, looking straight at her.

Mind sight.

Raeya was thinking of many things, I could

hear her mind voice in my head.

"I have a lot to teach her, about her gift, herbs, Noctua, and Elyon."

Raeya looked at me and grinned. But all of a sudden I couldn't hear her mindvoice anymore. I looked at Raeya.

"I am guessing that Jone did not block you when you trained," she mused.

"No, he didn't," I answered.

"Men," Raeya smirked, "You have many things to learn, and I will teach you all the things you need know."

SEVEN

Reading

We looked through the rest of the books, but did not find much more about my gift, it was all the same information. So we put them back and looked for mindvoicing books, and Raeya found Elyon's book, too.

We spread out the books on the table in piles, every day we would do a study about something in Elyon's book. Then study everything else, from mindvoice training and learning about healing herbs, to Noctua, my bonded wix, and more about my gift.

I also need to learn how to ride Noctua, and how to get up on her, for that matter. I wonder if Raeya could teach me that too…

"Me hope so." Noctua looked up at me with her big black eyes.

My thoughts were broken when I heard twittering and the opening of a door. I saw Raeya coming inside with Mentha zipping in behind her. Mentha landed on my hand, I sat up, for I was lying down on the sofa taking a rest, and listened to her tweets and squeaks.

I'd never been this close to Mentha before, I thought that she was all black, but her chest was a sunset orange, she had a dark scarlet throat, and her back and head were a blue-black iridescent color. Mentha took off and landed on a little nest in the top corner of the room, I hadn't noticed it, it was made out of mud and sticks.

"I went and picked some herbs that we can dry and make into an oil. I also picked some that we can put in dinner tonight." said Raeya cheerfully, "Come, and help me with dinner, I will also teach you how to cook some meals."

I walked to the kitchen with her.

She put the herbs on the table, "Oh…that's not good."

"What?" my eyes landed on one of the plants. It was turning black, only a little bit of green was left. "What's wrong with it?"

"It looks like I accidentally picked a bad one."

She grabbed it, but I caught her arm, "Wait, put it down. I want to try something."

She set it back on the table.

Elyon imi kuzon.

I laid my hand down on it, light came out of my finger tips. I smiled and pressed harder. The plant turned a bright a green then started glowing, the black disappeared. I took back my hand, green leaves dimming back down. I did it!

Raeya gasped, "That is the most amazing thing I have ever seen."

I grinned, "I was hoping it would work. I wasn't sure because it wasn't a creature, or maybe it was too far gone."

"Well done, Eleny." She touched the pale green stem. "Do you know how to cook anything?"

"My grandmother taught me how to make bread, and how to prepare and stuff chicken. I've known how to cook eggs and how to boil and season vegetables, too."

"Yes, but I will teach you much more,

including how to make pastato and those muffins."

"Jone Samb to Eleny Nil."

I gasped. *Welcome, it is nice to hear from you.*

"Hello Eleny dear, I was just checking on you, have you reached Raeya yet?"

I got here yesterday.

"Yesterday? How did you get there yesterday?"

I rescued a barn owl wix and now I'm her bonded, I flew on her from Way River to the peak where Raeya lives.

"My, my, you've been busy, have you not?"

Yep, and I've found out what gift I have and how to use it from the books Raeya has. We're about to start dinner now, she's going to teach me how to cook many things and hopefully she knows how to bake double fruit pie.

"My goodness, Me too, well I will let you get to cooking. Remember, if you ever need anything you have a place here in Shepla. Goodbye, my dear, and Elyon be with you!"

Good bye, Jone, and the same to you!

"Eleny? Are you alright?" I saw Raeya standing in front of me, waving her hands.

"Oh, sorry, Jone spoke to me and asked about my trip."

"Well, now that you're finished come over

here."

I went to her side and learned how to bake potatoes in the oven. When it was done cooking we stuffed them with butter, cheese, and herbs.

After we ate we went back to the books. We were going to learn about Noctua.

I found a book about birds and flipped through it, we finally found somethings about barn owls and I read aloud.

"They have extremely good hearing, with one ear higher than the other, being able to know exactly where a little rodent is on the ground by hearing it's tiny heartbeat. Their heart-shaped faces actually direct the sound to their ears, so that is why they turn their heads all the way around sometimes.

"They also can, of course, see in the dark. Better than in the light, actually. They have down on their wings and tail, feathers fine enough to stop the swoosh of the larger wing feathers, breaking down the wind currents so they are silent in flight."

By the time I was done reading the short page, Noctua was on the table listening intently.

"That why I hear so well?"

Yep, that's why.

"Me not know I could turn my head all around, either."

She stood up strait and slowly turned her head backwards to look at Raeya, who was behind her.

"Whoa, that feel weird."

I gave a laugh.

"Since that's pretty much it, let's start on herbs," Raeya smiled.

I nodded as Noctua flew out the window with Mentha, "Yeah, sure. You know, I think Noctua learned some things about herself that she didn't even know."

"I'm sure. Now there are many herbs that help headaches, stomachaches, nausea, and much more," Raeya said. We had cleaned up and it was mid afternoon, we had a medicine herb book out and Raeya was reading aloud.

"You might have to take this book with you, this is a lot of information. First there are chives, it keeps away bugs, make it into oil. Thyme, sore throat and stomach ache, by mouth. Lavender is for stress, sleep, and minor burn, also as oil."

She continued to tell me of many others like mint, ginger, aloe vera, rosemary, basil, and parsley. The book said what the plant did and how to prepare it.

Raeya was right, I just might have to take the book, or, at least, make a smaller copy of it.

Raeya continued, "Now it is time to get dinner and heat it up, it's in the springs and I must go and get it, I will be right back," she said, getting up.

"I'll come too, I haven't seen the springs yet," I followed her out the door.

I walked after Raeya through some trees and saw water coming out of the mountain, it created a little pool and a stream was flowing out of it. It was a beautiful sight, seeing the oak trees and pine trees with the setting sun shining over them. Everything had a golden glow, even the dark mountain wall.

Raeya picked up the food while I looked for Noctua with our bond. I looked around for the hollow Noctua had told me about. I finally saw it in a fir tree and looked inside, leaves and feathers were everywhere, making it nice and cozy, but she wasn't inside.

I frowned. *Where is she? Noctua, where are you?*

"Behind you."

As her high pitched, hooty voice spoke in

my head, I turned around and Noctua was in wix form, her white face now golden from the glow of the sun. Her wings were tucked because of the small space, but they were still a gorgeous golden with gray-blue spots and the same for her back and tail. Her beak was a pale peachy pink, like the morning sunrise.

Noctua walked closer to me and I scratched between her eyes, her favorite spot. I then smoothed the feathers on her neck, she nudged me with her smooth white horns.

So have you and Mentha been having a good time?

"Yes, she told me where air currents are and what they are, and how to ride them."

Wait, have you been out of the valley?

"Yes"

Could you have at least told me?

"Um, me will tell you next time?"

I went over to Raeya and helped her pick up the dinner, "Did you know that they went out?" I asked.

"Yes," Raeya answered.

I gave a scowl, "Well I didn't."

"I assumed that Noctua would have told you, I'm sorry, I would have if I knew," she said.

"Well, she didn't." I said, annoyed.

"Don't be so hard on her, remember she isn't used to having a bonded. How long has she been off on her own?"

"Six months."

"Well, can you imagine that for half of a year you would not have anyone to ask or tell that you are doing something?"

"I guess I can, I just..." I sighed and started to head back.

Raeya followed with Noctua and Mentha by her side, "You have lost so much already, you're just trying to protect her."

I sighed again, "Yeah."

We walked back to the house and ate the pastato for dinner.

Raeya was right.

EIGHT

The Box

It had been a moon since I'd come to Raeya's clearing. I had learned so much about my gift and Elyon's book. I learned how to use many herbs, and learned how to make salves, oils, and powders with them. I would keep them with me while I traveled. I also learned some human anatomy. The bones, organs, veins and arteries, and a whole lot more so I could focus on one part of the body instead of the whole when I was healing someone. Raeya's books helped me with all of it.

Raeya had also given me some riding clothes. Two women's blouses, a white one and a brown one, and two pairs of women breeches, one black, the other gray. These were very strange to me, for in Patera, women were not aloud to wear these types of clothing. But once I took off my dress and slipped into my new breeches, I fell in love with the comfortable garment immediately.

Raeya and I were feeding the noisy geese dinner when I heard a loud 'Maah!'

Raeya dropped the bucket with the corn and ran to the goats to look for Jane, the pregnant one. She wasn't with the others.

We ran to the barn and saw her lying down in the dirt, we went to her side, she was breathing slowly, too slow. Raeya looked up at me and said that the baby was coming, and that I needed to go get some towels. I ran to the house and grabbed as many as I could, then ran back.

I froze when I came to Raeya, she was crying. The mother was not moving, but I saw something moving in Raeya's arms and it was the cutest little brown and white goat, I gave her the towels.

I looked to Jane and gasped, she was breathing even slower than before.

I knelt down beside the limp body. I laid my hands down on her head.

Elyon imi kuzon.

The peace came and I transferred it to her, it felt like I stayed there for a few hours, but I couldn't tell. When I opened my eyes again Raeya was staring at me from the doorway then I looked at Jane, her eyes opened and she stood up slowly. The baby tried to stand, we watched it take its first steps. When it gained balance it hobbled over to its mother and started nursing.

"She is very thankful," Raeya walked over to me and gave me a hug, sniffling, "and I am too. You were there for at least an hour, I decided to let you do what you were doing and went to finish feeding the geese. Come, you must be tired, let us have some tea in the house."

I followed her to the cottage and went to the sofa and sat down. As I waited for Raeya to come back with the tea Noctua cuddled up on my chest.

I woke up with a jump, a clanking noise came from the kitchen. I was in my room, the plants by the window were freshly watered.

How did I end up in here?

I pulled back the covers, stood up, and opened the door. A delicious smell came to my nose, Raeya was over the sink washing dishes. She turned around and grinned.

"Ah, you are awake, when I came back with tea you had fallen asleep. Noctua helped me carry you to your room, did you sleep well?"

I nodded, "Yes, um, how long was I asleep?" I lifted myself to sit on the counter, which was quite high because it was built for a Xelman.

Raeya went back to scrubbing the dishes, "The rest of the evening, and night, you slept, it took a lot of energy to heal Jane when she was near death. The herb was quite small, but this took much more. As you grow you will find things out about your gift that is not in a book," she answered thoughtfully while scrubbing a bowl, "For example, I cannot talk to reptiles for too long without getting a headache, they have very sharp and loud mindvoices and sometimes they can't even communicate very well. I don't know if it is just me, or if it is for everyone with the nature gift, but it is not in a book." Raeya finished washing the last dish and pulled something out of the oven.

"Mm, what is it?" I smelled it.

"Cinnamon cake, with honey on top from a beehouse that is in this very valley," she said.

I jumped down and dragged a step stool to the counter then found some plates. We ate the delicious cake in the main room.

"Mm, delicious, we need to put this in the cookbook that we're making," I said as I finished the last bite on my plate.

"Yes, good idea, you have been getting better at cooking and baking, pretty soon you could make a good meal by yourself," said the old woman. We sat in silence for a moment.

"Raeya?"

"Yes?"

"Do you know how to bake double fruit pie? Jone baked it and I would like to learn how."

"No, I don't think I do, but it might be in an old book with recipes that I kept with me when I traveled. I found out how to make delicious delicacies from across Iyim, you are welcome to look there."

"Thank you." I stood.

After we cleaned up I went to my room and changed into my gray dress black boots. I then went to the library and found the book with the double fruit pie recipe, when I found it I wrote it down in my cookbook.

Then I found Raeya tending to the goats, the new baby in particular. When I came to the gate all of the kids came and said hello while I stepped through. Raeya was sitting down in the grass and I went and joined her. Talons grabbed my shoulder and glanced up as Noctua's golden wings glistened in the sunlight.

Hello.

"Hi, I think me ate all of mice and rats in shed so Raeya won't need to worry anymore."

Great! Where've you been while I was sleeping?

"Here and there, exploring the valley."

Anything interesting?

"I found beehouse Raeya talked about."

How did you know about the beehouse? You weren't present.

Noctua changed position so she could look at me.

Oh, I forgot that you heard my thoughts.

"Yes, well, it wasn't nice find, when I flew close they chased me until me was on the other side of valley."

That's not good.

I tried to hide my smile, but I knew she could hear my thoughts and so it didn't matter.

She was offended.

Sorry, Noctua, but the thing is, you can't really get stung by the bees.

"I'd never met the awful things before, so me don't know what to think."

I giggled, and Raeya glanced at me with a questioning expression, I just smiled and looked at Noctua. Raeya nodded as if she knew why I had giggled.

"I want you to have something," she said, pulling a small box, the size of the palm of my hand, out of her dress, "a brilliant man gave this to me, he understood the way Elyon made things, and he captured the light waves in the air, the color bands, the molecules in different liquids, and so many other things."

We stood up and I followed Raeya out of the goat pen and into a field, she set the box on the ground and pressed a button on the side. The box opened up and started unfolding, and kept unfolding until it became a whole wall! It was about a foot higher than me and three yards wide, with cupboards, drawers, and even a wardrobe to hang dresses, capes and coats.

I stood astonished, wide-eyed, and mouth hanging. Raeya pointed at a cabinet and opened it, mist flowed out. I looked and there inside it was covered in ice. I stared at it until Raeya started telling me what it was,

"It is like my stream, it keeps food and drink cold," she said. She then closed it and opened the wardrobe, it was deeper than I thought, five feet at least. I was glad that there were hangers hanging at the top so my dress wouldn't get wrinkled. Raeya pointed to many drawers for garments, cupboards for dishes, and even a place to hang hats. I was amazed at it all.

"Now it is time to fill it," Raeya said.

"I'll go get my things!" I said in excitement, running to the cottage, it was not far away, just a hundred yards at most. Noctua flew off and headed back to Raeya, she was so light and quiet, that I kept forgetting that she was there.

I went to my room and grabbed my rose sack and filled it with my garments, maps and compass, and my blanket. When I came back Raeya was sitting in a wooden chair, Noctua sitting on the arm.

"Where did you get the chair?" I asked quizzically.

"The wardrobe of course," she pointed, "there is a whole table set in there, I am giving it to you. The set is for travel, the chairs and table fold tightly so they are small and can fit without taking much space. Now let's pack it full," she chuckled, standing up.

The tall, old, woman folded the chair a certain way, which I watched intently so I wouldn't forget how, then she put it in the wardrobe. Noctua then came and landed on my shoulder again, taking interest in what I was doing. I took out one thing at a time, putting my blankets in a cabinet first, then my extra clothes in the wardrobe.

Every now and then I'd hear an "Ooo" or "Aah" from Noctua, gazing at my things.

When I finished with that I found a drawer to store my gray shoes that were for social events, I had been wearing my boots around the little animal farm so I would not get them dirty.

When I put my maps and compass away Raeya came and pushed a button at the bottom of the wall and it started folding smaller and smaller until it was a box again.

Raeya picked it up and looked at me, "Another way to do it is simpler, if it is full you just hold it and say what you want then push the button," she said, then passed it to me.

"What does it do?" I asked, using my finger to trace the delicate design.

"You'll see."

I looked at her skeptically then said, "shoes" to the box then pressed the button. It started to unfold, but only to the size of the drawer I had put my shoes in. I gasped and pulled it out, inside were my gray shoes.

"Whoa!" I said, smiling, "that will be easier to deal with when I travel."

"Yes, I used it when I traveled," Raeya agreed, "I'm glad I didn't have to unfold the entire wall, instead just a section of it, here, close it then give it to me a moment, please," she said, holding out her hand. I watched the drawer fold up after I pressed the button, then gave it to Raeya.

She spoke into it, "Cold box, breeches," then set it down in the green grass. The box started unfolding but only to the point of the cold box and the drawer with my breeches in it.

"You can do two or three at a time instead, it doesn't take as long," she said, pressing the button, then handing it back to me, "Also, it will still work even if it gets wet, and the things inside it will be dry. So if it rains, or you fall into the water, it won't break."

"Thank you, this is wonderful!" I exclaimed.

"Let's eat, after all of this excitement, I've gotten hungry," she said.

We walked back to the house and ate the leftover pastato for dinner then went to bed. Noctua, this time, cuddled up to my neck on the pillow.

I could hardly believe all the interesting and marvelous things I had discovered since my journey began. I wondered what tomorrow would bring.

NINE

New Meetings

I was with Noctua, sitting under a tree on my cape and reading a book about wixes that Raeya gave me.

Noctua was in my lap, cuddled up in a ball of feathers asleep, I stroked her head and she gave a little cooing whistle. Green light shined down on us through the leaves as the breeze blew by. When I was reading a part about wixens Raeya contacted me.

"Raeya Pinsa to Eleny Nil."

Welcome.

"Come to the cottage quickly."

Without warning the connection cut off, she sounded urgent. I picked up Noctua softly and set her in her hollow then took off running to the cottage. The tall grass brushed my breeches. One with thorns snagged them.

"Ow!" I unsnagged it and kept running.

Elyon imi kuzon.

Those words popped up in my mind so easily now.

I came to the door, bursting in. Raeya was sitting at the table with two men, they stood up and turned their attention on me. I shifted my weight from one foot to the other, fiddling with my fingers. I regained my composure and walked briskly toward the table, trying to calm my haggard breathing.

Raeya gestured to the men and introduced me, "This is Grimblon Bend," she pointed to a stout middle-aged Thasfaen with dark blond hair, dark blue eyes, and tan skin, I gave a shy wave and curtsied, which was strange to do with breeches on.

Then she continued, "and this is Alexovin Hendruton," she pointed to the other man, he was a young Xelman, but taller than Raeya, so way taller than me, I had to look up to see his face.

I curtsied again and he bowed a little, "Call me Alex," he said.

I smiled a tiny smile and nodded.

"This is Eleny Nil, she came here to learn about herbs," said Raeya, pointing to me.

I noticed she didn't tell them about my gift, or that I had mindvoicing abilities. I took a seat at the table. Inside I was embarrassed, I thought that Raeya needed me badly.

I mindvoiced her, *Eleny Nil to Raeya Pinsa.* "Welcome."

You couldn't have told me about them? I thought you were hurt or something.

"I apologize, dear, they just knocked, and I thought it was you. But then I realized it wasn't you and I got flustered because normally people tell me when they are coming."

Raeya looked guiltily at her hands, I took a deep breath to calm down.

Then mindvoiced again. *Why didn't you tell them about my gifts?*

"Because that is your information to tell."

The men sat when Raeya did and they started to tell us why they were here and Raeya cut off the connection.

Grimblon spoke first, "You have probably heard of the raids going on in Iyim," he said, and we nodded.

"I've been through one in Shepla," I said.

"I'm afraid we've been through a few as well, we've just come from Waterway, stayed there for about two weeks, we took a beating, and helped all we could. The men in black have chased us ever since and we sought refuge here. We're very sorry for intruding," Grimblon explained.

"Of course, any of Elyon's Men are welcome here, but what is puzzling me is how did you know this place was here?" Raeya asked them.

Alright, I just had to know. *Eleny Nil to Raeya Pinsa.*

"Welcome. Again."

What is Elyon's Men?

"They follow Elyon and serve Him by telling people about Him and how He loves them. They also help the people going through hardships, now shh, listen."

I cut the connection and listened to the men.

Grimblon continued, "We have been going to the different towns of Iyim, except in Patera, like we do every year. We started in Portum, then went to Urbs, Pago, then to little villages along the way to The Falls. When we reached Shepla we saw Jone Samb and he told us about your valley and said that it was safe here. We continued on to Waterway, that was where the raid was. They chased us out and kept chasing us until we lost them in the mounts. We then came to you," he finished, looking out of breath.

Alex spoke up, "Um, Mrs. Bend is here, and not meaning to intrude, but she would like to sleep in a house rather than outside for once," he said sheepishly.

Raeya looked up, "Yes of course, where is she?"

"Sitting on the front porch."

"Eleny, please be a dear and let her in, I'll start dinner. You make our guests comfortable."

I stood up and went to the porch, I found a Thasfaen woman sitting in the rocking chair.

"Hello, I'm Eleny Nil, would you like to come in, Mrs. Bend?" I asked.

She stood up and smiled, "Yes I would, but please, just call me Teamalie," she curtsied, and I did back. Teamalie's hair was a reddish auburn color, with olive green eyes, and although she was a tiny bit stout, too, she was very pretty. I opened the door and led her in.

"Please make yourselves comfortable," I said, gesturing to the sofa and cushioned chairs. Teamalie sat on the sofa and her husband joined her. Alexovin chose a chair. There were a few packs on the floor near the door.

When they were settled I went to the kitchen to see what I could help Raeya with. She said that she didn't need any so I went to talk with the Thasfaens and Xelman, but only Alex was there.

I sat down, trying to look regal and composed. "So, where are you going next?" I asked, trying to start up a conversation.

"Wix Town next, there we meet more of Elyon's Men, and women, and we all travel together," said Alex, "after that we go into the rest of The Plains then into Aridon and Minnek."

"Why not Patera?" I said, "Aren't there people there that need Elyon, too?"

He looked down, "They attack people who try to bring His Word to them, eventually we stopped trying."

"Oh," I looked at him, his face was grim, his eyes were a super pale green, and his hair was shiny black, which made his skin look even paler.

"How did *you* end up here?" he asked, looking up.

"I used to live in Polos with my grandmother, one night a woman came with a baby who had," I caught myself.

Can I trust him? He feels different than the other two. Almost like Raeya's feeling. Maybe its a Xelman thing.

To Paterans it's illegal to help a mother escape with a gifted. But he is one of Elyon's Men, so he can be trusted, right?

"Who had what?" Alex pulled me out of thought.

My eyes thinned to lines, "Can I trust you?"

"Yes," he said, rolling his eyes.

I took a breath, I hoped this was what Elyon wanted. "He had a gift, and I helped his mother get out of Patera and we went our separate ways in Shepla," I said slowly, "I don't know what became of her after that."

I told him I met Jone, that I have mindvoicing abilities, and how I got to Raeya's valley, although I didn't tell him of my gift.

When I finished there was a few minutes of silence, then I heard a hair raising screech. It looked like Alex did too, because he jumped up and headed to the door.

I tried to stop him, but he was already outside. Following, I knew that it was Noctua eating.

Do you have to screech like that every time you hunt?

"Yes, it scares animals out of hiding, so me can catch it if it under something."

After you eat it come here, the new people need to know it's only you, not someone dying. I mind giggled.

"Me coming, the animal got away, someone scared it wrong way before me catch it."

I rolled my eyes. The sun was still up in the sky, so I could see pretty well. I stepped onto the porch, Alex already in the yard.

Talons grabbed my shoulder.

"Wait, Alex!" I called, "It was just my barn owl wix, the one I told you about."

"Oh," he looked relieved, but a little bit embarrassed, I could see a tint of pink come into his cheeks.

Noctua turned her gaze to Alex. *"Ooh, he is handsome."*

I have to agree with that.

"Handsomer than old man who had wrinkles you

mindvoiced to."

I stifled a laugh. *You're right.*

As Alex walked back up I apologized and started walking to the goats, "Would you like me to show you around?" I asked, turning to look at him.

"Sure."

When we reached the pen I told him who was who. Then we went to the rest of the animals, the springs, and an herb patch I had found.

When the sun was soon about to set we headed back to the cottage. I walked in with Noctua on my shoulder, as usual, and Alex close behind me, along with his cool presence.

Raeya had brought the food to the table and the Thasfaen couple were already seated. Noctua flew off and landed on the back of an empty chair. I took the seat she was perched on and took a biscuit from a bowl.

I glanced up and noticed that the couple were staring at Noctua.

She turned around and stared at them right back and blinked. *"Why they're looking at me funnily?"*

They haven't met you yet Noctua.

She turned her head to me, seeming puzzled, as if barn owls were the most common thing to see.

I swallowed my food and smiled sweetly at the Bends, "This is Noctua, she's a barn owl wix. If she worries you I guess I can send her outside."

"Oh, no, she's just beautiful in bird form, that's all. Noctua, is it?" said Teamalie, and I nodded.

She says you're beautiful, Noctua.

"Oh, me like her, tell her I say thank you."

Noctua nudged my head with her beak then tried to look regal and elegant, which she was flawless at.

"She says thank you," I told her, "and that she likes you, too."   Mrs. Teamalie smiled at Noctua.

Remembering the food, we prayed to Elyon then ate and Mr. Bend told us of stories that happened when he traveled.

When he finished Raeya and I cleaned up, then she showed the guests to other rooms I had no idea were there.

After they were settled Raeya and I went to bed, exhausted from the visit.

TEN

Racing and Fun

The next day I went to eat breakfast early in the morning, when Noctua was the most energetic. We had been training on how to ride higher in altitude and she needed a lot of energy for this.

I knew that it would be kind of rude to do it, with guests and all, but I had promised Noctua that we would do this days ago, and she was at the top of my priority list.

I dragged the foot stool to a cabinet and

stepped up on it.   Noctua, who was sitting on my shoulder, eagerly shuffled, excited that we were going to have a picnic up on one of the mountain ledges.   When I brought out some sweet bread I heard the door behind me open. Turning around slowly, I saw it was Alex.

"Good morning," he said, "You're up early, but I guess you have to wake earlier than normal here. With all the animals to take care of."

"Good morning, and yes I do have to wake up earlier here, but I don't feed the animals, I only help Raeya sometimes." I paused, "Noctua and I are going to practice going up even higher than we have been flying. Then we're going to have a picnic. I apologize for leaving while you are here. I just have been promising Noctua for a while now." I picked up some more sweet bread and handed it to him.   He took it gently from my hand, his was twice the size of mine. Now that I was on the stool my head was level with his, I could see that his eyes weren't just pale green, but had flecks of silver in them.

He took it, and grinned a little, "Thanks. That sounds fun, you haven't had your wix for long?"

"No, not really," shaking the strange, yet

embarrassing, feeling away.

I took some different bread and brought it down then took my little box out and spoke into it, barely a whisper. It opened up to just the size of the cupboard I stored food in.

Now I just need to go get some cheese from the springs.

"See you later," I said to Alex.

"Oh, see you, too."

As I went to the door his stare burned into my neck, then I walked across the porch, towards the hollow Noctua had claimed.

She went when I was busy, where the springs were. When I reached the springs Noctua went to the little hole in the tree. I bent down to retrieve the box which held the food and drink. Grabbing the cheese, I decided to bring some meat for Noctua, too.

When I had everything packed in my box, Noctua's screech came to my ears.

"What're you? This my hollow, not yours!"

What's the matter?

"Eleny, something in my hollow! It scared me!"

I ran to the hollow to find Noctua flustered, wings extended, looking at something covered in straw.

Elyon imi kuzon.

I stuck my hand in and uncovered it, surprised that it didn't try to get away. It was a little bird, about a third of the size of Noctua. I breathed, unaware I was holding my breath.

I picked it up, it had big black eyes on both sides of it's flat head, its feathers were many mottled shades of browns and grays. It had a white throat and long black tail feathers with a white stripe across them. It had a wide, short beak. It was actually quite cute.

"It's alright little one," I said to the small creature, "I won't hurt you. My, you gave us a fright!"

It's eyes locked with mine, the big shiny spheres looked as though they would pop out if they widened even a tiny bit more.

I heard some ruffling behind me and turned around quickly. It was Alex, he looked out of breath.

"Is everything alright?" I asked, worried.

He looked at my hand that held the bird. The animal saw Alexovin and jumped out of my hand, flying to the young Xelman. "This is Deiless," he said, seeing my confused face, "Uh, he's a wix too. A nighthawk wix."

"You didn't say you had a wix."

"You never asked." He smiled, patting the brown bird's head.

"He scared Noctua half to death," I giggled, "she had no idea he was in her hollow."

"I think *she* scared Deiless even more," he said, a look of realization appearing on his face, then it turned sheepish, "Oh, you mean that was Noctua's hollow? I had no idea, not knowing if Raeya was wix friendly, I told him to find a place to sleep for the night."

"It's fine, Noctua sleeps with me in the house." I said, having to tilt my head to look up at him, now that I was on the ground. "She only comes here when I'm doing something boring, so she goes and explores then comes to eat. But if you want I'm sure that Raeya would let him stay inside during the night, like Mentha and Noctua do."

"Mentha?"

"Raeya has a barn swallow wix, though she's normally shy and is most of the time in her nest, which is in the corner of the ceiling."

Alexovin smiled again, revealing shiny white teeth, "Oh, then that answers that. At first I thought that it was the dirt clingers' hive."

I chuckled.

Noticing that the sun was getting higher in the sky, I called Noctua. Two seconds later she landed on my shoulder. Noctua's hooty voice popped up in my head. *"Let's take them with us up high!"*

Are you sure?

"Yes, yes, yes! Me didn't know he was wix 'til a bit ago. When you talked to Xelman me been talking to Deiless."

Oh. Really? I guess we could invite them.

"Yay! I want to get know him and you can get to know the Xelman."

I looked at Alex, he must have been talking to Deiless.

"Noctua really wants to get to know Deiless," I said, probably interrupting a conversation, "I guess, well," I blushed, "would you want to come with us?" Where was this blushing coming from? *Go away!*

"Sure, we'll come, if it's no trouble. From the kind we already caused, I would think you'd want to get away from us."

"Oh no, it's no trouble, I just need to get some food for an extra Xelman and wix."

"No need to give Deiless food, he eats

insects.

I nodded while I got some more cheese.

Then he said, "It's funny how wixes like to get to know each other right when they meet, I wish that people were that way sometimes."

"Yeah," I said, standing up, "I agree."

Noctua flew off of my shoulder and landed on the ground. The wispy, golden, light surrounded her, getting brighter and bigger until it faded. Replacing the owl was a mystical wix.

"Ready to go?" I asked him, while patting Noctua's shoulder.

He put down Deiless. The light flowing around him was darker than Noctua's. More like a silvery bronze.

Whoa.

Replacing the little ruddy creature was a charming wix, who was so much bigger, and bulkier than Noctua, that you could see his muscles rippling. (He may have been stronger, but I thought Noctua was prettier.) His beak and horns were a dark gray, his tail and wings were black and on the underside of his wings was gray with one white stripe across each, just like he had in bird form. His throat was white, his head a shiny brown, his back and legs a shadowy silver.

"He's beautiful!" I exclaimed.

"So is she," he pointed at Noctua, "I've never met a barn owl wix, I hear they're rare."

I jumped up on Noctua like Raeya had shown me a few days ago and grabbed onto Noctua's long, soft, feathers, glowing with pride that Noctua was the wix that chose me.

Did you hear that Noctua,? He says you're rare.
"Me am?"
Yeah. Okay, Noctua, let's go.
"Let's go, let's go!"

Her wings started pumping, flapping faster and faster. She then crouched down and jumped up in the air at break-neck speed. She would not have done this had I not been trained how to hold on, lean down, and lift my shoulders up to protect my neck from getting whiplash. Raeya and Mentha had taught us the trick, it helped get us up in the air easier and quicker. We were above the trees in seconds.   I looked down. *Where did Alexovin go?*

"I no see him."

He wasn't down in the little springs clearing.

"Hey!"

I searched around, he was directly behind me.

"Come on!" I called and waved my free hand, "Follow us!"

Noctua flew higher and higher, until we could see out of the valley, out over the mountains were fields of green grass, little farm houses, and the edge of Shadow Forest.

Noctua found an air current and zoomed into it. The cool air whisked through my hair. My hands held on tight to the thick fur of Noctua's hide when her wings stopped flapping and tucked in. The fur was not only something to hold onto, but it also acted as a saddle, holding me in place.

We were falling head first, my stomach as if it was being squeezed like lemons for lemonade, but a split second before we hit the mountain she spread her enormous wings. When flying back up, she glided over the terrain.

I turned around and laid back on Noctua's neck, watching the wing muscles loosen and tighten. Noctua told me when we reached the highest altitude we have ever been.

I sat up, backwards, and saw Deiless gliding behind us. *Hey, slow down for a second.*

She stopped flapping so fast and Alex caught up.

"Hello," I said to him, turning back around.

"Hi, nice dive."

"Thanks." I smiled.

"Do you want to do something fun?" he said, grinning.

"Sure, why not?"

"Follow me!" leaning over, he suddenly fell down.

"Alexovin!"

Deiless dived down, chasing him.

"You do same! I catch you, too!"

Okay...

Looking down I started to slide off, scared out of my mind. Why was I doing this? I had no idea, but I let go of Noctua's feathers anyway.

I screamed, searching for Alex. He was below me, upside down, looking at me and smiling. He spread out his arms and legs so the air would catch him, then he did a few flips.

I smiled when I saw Noctua come up beside me.

"You having fun?"

I guess!

But when she came close enough I grabbed onto her so we were both falling headfirst.

Let's find a place to land.

Her wings spread out and, again, we glided

over the mounts. I saw a large ledge.

There!

"Me see it."

She went and landed.

Jumping off of her back, I scanned the mountains for Deiless's silvery hide. But with the mountains as a background, he would be camouflaged. I kept searching.

When I saw movement, I turned my head that way. There they were. I waved my hands in the air. He saw me and came to the ledge. When he landed I had already brought out a blanket and the food from my box.

When Alex saw it he put on the most confused face I had ever seen when I pressed the button and the box folded up.

"What in the world was that?" he asked.

As he sat down, I told him about the box. I took a piece of cheese and bread and set it on a plate when I was done explaining.

"That's great, makes it easier to travel, doesn't it?"

"Yeah, it does."

I took a bite of my cheese, Noctua was in my lap eating the piece of meat I brought for her. I glanced at the young Xelman. "So, Alex, I've told you about me, what about you? First of all, how old are you?"

He looked a little reluctant but opened up, "Seventeen, I've been Grimblon's apprentice since I was ten, that was when I learned of Elyon." He looked out over the valley, "Grimblon and his family were taking a trip, sharing about Elyon. I decided to join them. How old are you?"

"Sixteen. I turn seventeen in half a moon. So you just kept traveling with the Bends, as one of Elyon's Men?"

"Yep, I craved adventure, but eventually was able to start participating more when I grew older."

Deiless, who was flying around in circles around us grabbed my attention, "How did you meet Deiless?"

"On one trip, a few years ago, I found him washed up on the shore of a river. He looked dead, but when I bent down to take a closer look, I saw that he was breathing. I nurtured him back to health, and when he woke up, I found out he was a wix. A big surprise, I thought that I was going crazy when a bird starting to speak."

"It sounds sort of like my story. Is it like a test or something? To see what the person does?"

"I don't know. It's a mystery." He shrugged.

I giggled, thinking of Noctua and her quirks, how she said 'me' instead of 'I' sometimes, and also mixed up her words.

"Does Deiless have his own way of speaking?" I wondered.

"Well, he says things backwards sometimes, when he says something like, 'Help me' he means 'Me help'," Alex snorted, "So when it's confusing, I need to look at the situation. When Noctua found him in that hollow, he screamed, 'I help need!' and I've gotten used to his speaking so I knew something was wrong. I used my ability to get to him and-"

"Wait, wait. I just figured it out. That's what it is, you can mindvoice!" *And why didn't he tell me this?*

"Um, no."

"Yes, you do." I gasped, he gave off the same feeling Raeya and Jone did. "That's what that feeling was! I knew there was something different about you!" I then could tell that he was hiding his emotions.

I crossed my arms and glared at him, "Admit it. You *can* mindvoice, and now I know." I then smiled.

"Fine, yes, not many people know, and I like to keep it that way." He glared back at me.

"Oh." Surprised, I said, "Why?"

"I just don't, that's all."

Um, okay...

"That is strange."

I looked at Noctua, she hopped towards Alex. He seemed uncomfortable under her chilly gaze.

"I sense fear in him."

Well, it's his information to tell, as Raeya said.

"Well, do you ever mindvoice to anyone?" I took a bite of bread.

"No, not really." But he gave a hint of a grin, "Just my little brother, we both inherited it from my grandfather."

My mouth turned up, too, "You have a brother?"

He smirked, "Yes, a little rascal brother, he's thirteen and proud of it."

"I wish I had siblings. Does he miss you when you go on journeys?"

"Yes, he says one day he will come with me, that maybe next year. Grimblon and Teamalie travel all year long, but I only do for about nine to eleven moons."

"Whoa, you're home only up to three moons? That's not very long."

"Well, I enjoy what I do. Seeing people come to Elyon, watching their faces light up, their lives changed. It's amazing to see."

"It sounds like it."

A moment of silence.

"Perl is also like a little sister to me."

"Perl, who's that?"

"Oh, you didn't know that Grimblon and Teamalie had a daughter?"

I shook my head.

"She's sixteen, too. Perlelia is her full name. Do you remember when I said that we're going to meet some more people at Wix Town?"

I nodded.

"They normally all travel together, but this time the group split up so they could cover more cites. All of them met up at Portum then went to Urbs, then Pago, where I live, and also where we split up. They went to the rest of the villages throughout Shadow Forest while we went to Shepla. But Perl went with the others because they have little ones that they need help with." He took a breath, "That's about it."

I started to pick up, we had finished eating

and Noctua was getting restless. Putting the blanket back in the box, Noctua came and landed on my shoulder.

"We go now?"

Yep, you can transform now.

She flew and a burst of light shined and dim rapidly.

I didn't know that you could do it so fast!

"Me like when people go saying, 'Ooh' or 'Whoa!'"

You little rat!

I stifled a snort, jumped up on her, and saw that Alex was getting on Deiless.

"Come on, race you back!" he challenged, racing away.

I took off, following.

ELEVEN

Review and Reinforce

When we reached the cottage it was half past noon. I sent Noctua off to eat and Alex did the same to Deiless. The Bends were out on a walk and Raeya was in the living room, reading a book.

"Ah! Let's start on your lessons," she insisted, when she saw us come in, "What would you like to do first?"

"*Raeya Pinsa to Eleny Nil.*"

Welcome.

"Did you tell him about your gift and

mindvoicing?"

I didn't tell him about my gift, it just didn't feel right, but I did about the mindvoicing, don't worry, he mindvoices, too. But don't tell anyone I told you.

"Alright."

"Let's start with mindvoicing," Raeya decided, cutting the connection.

I looked at Alex. *Eleny Nil to Alexovin Hendruton.*

He sighed. *"Welcome."*

Would you like to train with me? I know how to do it well, but Raeya wants me to keep practicing anyways.

"Is she trustworthy?"

Why are you so worried?

"I have my reasons. But since you have told her about your ability then I guess I can."

He was hesitant, but told Raeya, "I have mindvoicing abilities."

"Oh, you do? I thought you might, you give off a mindvoicing feel," she said, "Would you like to join us?"

He grunted, "I guess."

"Today, unlike you think, Eleny, we are going to learn something new. I'm going to teach you how to listen in on someone's conversation."

Huh, I didn't know that you could do that.

"I know you didn't, that is why I am telling you about it."

Hey, that was Raeya's voice! How did she do that without permission?

She must have seen my face, "Yes, also how to do that. You don't specifically need to ask permission, it is just the right thing to do. Intruding and listening to other people's thoughts is rude, unless it is someone evil and you need to see if they are planning anything to hurt you. Now, I am going to mindvoice to Alexovin-"

"Alex," interrupted the Xelman.

"Yes, Alex," She nodded at him, "I am going to mindvoice Alex and you are going to try and listen in."

"Okay," I said, "Tell me when you're ready."

I realized I wouldn't get an answer. *I did once listen in on Raeya's thoughts for training, maybe it would be sort of like this.* I looked at the Xelmans.

Mindsight.

Voices popped up in my head. First Raeya's. *"So, how was your trip so far?"*

"We have had a good time, although I hope the other group didn't go through a raid."

"Yes, me too, where are they now?"

"In Shadow Forest, walking from village to village.

They might already be heading toward Wix Town."

I decided to join in.

Hey! I can hear you loud and clear.

Raeya turned her sight at me and chortled, her voice came to my head.

"Well done! We are now having a three-way conversation. Now Alex," She faced him. *"Eleny and I are going to talk, you are going to try and listen, and Eleny will try and block you."*

"Yes ma'am."

We cut off the connection, and I contacted Raeya.

Eleny Nil to Raeya Pinsa.

"Welcome. You don't need to ask permission if you were already talking to the person a moment earlier."

Oh.

"Hurry, block Alex, do not let him hear your thoughts as we are talking."

Elyon imi kuzon, Elyon imi kuzon.

"Try not to send me that thought, we need to be talking."

Did you sleep well last night?

She gave me a 'really?' look.

It was the only thing that came to mind, alright?

"Yes I did, did you?"

I did.

A pressure appeared on my temples.

I feel like something's squeezing my head.

"That's how you know someone is trying to listen to your thoughts or conversation. Now, block him."

I closed my eyes and kept thinking 'Elyon imi kuzon' without sending the thought to Raeya. The pressure eased when I did this, making it easier to concentrate.

"I think that is enough, let's see what Alex picked up."

I opened my eyes and Raeya looked up at Alex, "Now, did you hear anything?"

"No, but I did catch a crackled 'sleep well'."

"Good, but Eleny," she turned her gaze to me, "Next time you need to try harder. Now it is time for Eleny to look over her herbs, I'm going to give her a test to see if she remembered everything so far."

"I'll leave it to you ladies, then," He stood up, "See you later."

"Bye," I waved a little.

"Now let's go to the table," offered the old woman, standing up, "This is going to be difficult, we need to know that if you go on a journey you would know the plant, what it is for, and how to prepare it."

"I remember what everything is for, and I also made a booklet just in case I forget," I stated, showing her a little book that could fit in my cape pocket.

"And what if you lose it?" she glanced at me, I shrugged.

"That is why you are going to memorize everything."

I had to admit, she was stubborn. Sitting down, I pulled my long brown hair across my shoulder and started to re-braid it. Raeya opened a book, flipping through the pages, "Now, let's see here. Lavender."

"Hmm, lavender, it helps reduce stress and you prepare it as an oil."

"Correct, now mint."

Mint. Mint mint mint. What to do with mint.

Noctua's high-pitched voice popped in my head.

"Meant? Meant for what?"

No, no. Mint, it's an herb and I am trying to remember what to do with it.

"Oh, okay."

Raeya pulled me out of thought, "Eleny?"

"Oh, um, you can make it tea, oil, dry it, or eat it fresh for headache and nausea relief."

"Correct, now, basil and rosemary."

"Basil, for pain relief and makes bugs go away, prepare as oil. Rosemary, also for stress and stomach ache, and you can... you eat it fresh?"

"No, rosemary needs to be prepared as an oil or dried for the fragrance." Raeya smiled, loving when she was right, "See, you need to know them by heart."

I nodded.

She continued, "Thyme?"

"Thyme, prepare as tea for a sore throat."

"Yes, now sage."

"For insect bites and infection?"

"Yes, but as what?" she caught sight of my scrunched up nose, I was trying to remember.

"As an oil? Oh, and you can dry it to improve moods?"

"Well done, I love the smell of sage, it's very calming."

We continued to go through more herbs and flower plants.
When we were done Raeya put the book away and came back. We sat in silence for a while and I receded into deep thought. Raeya pulled me out of thought again when she sat up and looked straight at me, folding her hands on the table.

"Eleny, you have been here for quite some time, almost a whole moon in fact, and I feel that it would be best for you to go with Elyon's Men when they leave."

I was speechless. *Does she not want me here anymore?*

"Me hope she wants us."

I loved it when Noctua spoke out of nowhere.

Raeya explained, "You can't live here forever, dear, and I believe that Elyon gave you this chance. You know Elyon's Men are good people, and they can help your faith in Him grow."

"See, she does want us here."

Raeya picked up a book from her lap, gently set it down on the table, and slid it to me. "This is Elyon's Book. I have but a few, but I want you to have this one."

I grinned, reaching for the ancient book. "Thank you so much," I gasped. "But what about you? I can't just leave!"

"Yes, Eleny, you can and will. The Bends are leaving tomorrow to meet the other group, and if you want to ever see the world, this is the time to do it, when you are young." The ends of her lips turned up. "I have seen your face whenever they spoke of leading people to Elyon. It lights up every time they bring up the subject.

"You know that you want to go and show Him to them. And I found that the Bends also have a daughter who is your age. I am sure that you two would get along just fine."

"I guess, but I will talk to you often while I am away," I promised.

"Yes, and I will always answer."

Beaming, I knew she would keep her word, too. We went to the kitchen and started cooking. When we were done Raeya said to go see where our new friends were.

I skipped outside and found them talking at a table by the pond. The warm breeze was welcoming. The sun was starting to fall behind the mountains, giving a golden light. I strode up to them, the trees were creating shadows on their faces. But I noticed that the men weren't very happy. In fact, they looked like they were arguing.

"Hello, Raeya and I have just finished dinner, would you like to join us?" I asked, pulling them out of the conversation.

Teamalie looked up at me and grinned, "Of course!" she stood up, stepped over the bench, and linked her arm in mine, "These two men are boring me, you know with all the hunting talk. Let's go inside." She pulled me along.

I don't think that was really *what they were talking about. I guess I'll let it slide for now.*

"Hmm, me be watching them."

I looked up at Noctua, who was sitting in a pine tree. *Okay.*

We stepped through the door, Raeya had already set the table. Teamalie sat in a chair, followed by Raeya. Right when I dragged a seat back to sit I heard a knocking at the window behind the sofa. Pulling back the curtain, Noctua, perched on the sill, knocked again. She hopped up and down, that was when I noticed that Deiless was next to her, shy.

I thought you were going to watch the others.

"Me change my mind."

Opening the window, Noctua landed on my shoulder, and Deiless landed on my forearm. I set them on a cushioned chair then I sat back down at the dining table.

"Who is that," Raeya smiled, leaning over to see the little brown wix, "That little bird?"

"His name is Deiless, he's Alex's nighthawk wix," Teamalie answered.

"Ah," Raeya then scooped some of the dish

onto her plate, "Will the men join us?"

"No," said the Thasfaen, "They were deep in conversation, they might stay out there for a while."

"Then we shall cover the food and leave it out when we are finished," Raeya handed Teamalie a pot full of boiled carrots, "let's thank Elyon." We bowed our heads.

"Elyon, thank you for the food you have provided. Thank you for new friends that have come to stay with Eleny and I," Raeya glanced at Teamalie, "I ask you to give them safe passage though rough areas, so that they can share your word and fellowship with others. Let it be so."

Teamalie and I also said, "Let it be so."

Teamalie served herself some purple potatoes and I forked some of the chicken.

When we finished eating Teamalie helped in the kitchen, then went outside as Raeya and I sat in the living room. Noctua, who was in my lap in a ball of fluff, gave a few whistles while sleeping.

I was reading the book about wixes again, starting where I left off, when the Bends and Alex came in.

Teamalie sat by me on the sofa. I noticed, when she observed me, that she had very warm eyes, the dark green reminded me of the green leaves of Grandmother's roses back home. I sighed, my eyes burning.

Teamalie spoke, "We, Grimblon, Alex, and I, have come to a decision." She took my hand and gave a little smile, "We would like you to accompany us on our journey."

I bit my lip, "Actually, I am glad that you asked," my mouth curved into a smile, "Raeya and I have actually been wondering if I could go with you."

I looked up at Alex, he was grinning, Grimblon nodded, and Teamalie beamed, "How wonderful!" she squeezed my hands, "We will stay here for a few more days then go straight to Wix Town. I know that you and Perlelia will get along just wonderfully."

I hope. Oh Elyon let it be so.

TWELVE

A New Journey

    I didn't sleep much the nights after learning that I was going to leave.

    I had gotten used to waking up early and feeding the animals.

    Playing with the goats and holding the chicks and ducklings.

    Eating breakfast out in the garden with the birds tweeting all around me.

    Flying above the rich colors of flowers of the valley.

Helping Raeya bake and cook all of her childhood treats.   Reading books about herbs and wixes and my gift in Raeya's little library. Well, if I *found* anything of my gift.

Now, in my bed looking up at the ceiling and trying to fall asleep, I just realized how much I was going to miss this little bedroom full of plants. Even though I'd not been here that long, this little valley had become my home. I had nowhere else to go, except for Jone's of course. But Raeya had been like my grandmother away from grandmother. I missed Grandmother so. And *now* I was also leaving *Raeya*.

The next day I would be traveling with people I barely knew. But I guess Raeya had trusted them, and I trust Raeya, so I should at least try to trust them, too.

Raeya had been filling my little box with all sorts of things today. Mostly books, then herbs, food, clothes, salves, bandages, blankets, and a feather pillow that she gave me. She scurried through out the house, gathering items. I didn't see half the stuff she put in from how fast she was going.

This time I would be prepared and could even, if something happened, live in the wilderness for a few weeks with all of my supplies.

Finally, while pondering on all of this, I drifted into sleep.

I stood up groggily, stretched, and stepped over to the plants then watered them for the last time that I knew of. After dressing into my tan blouse, gray breeches, and cape, I slipped my feet into stockings and put my boots on.

When I came to the kitchen Raeya was leaning against the counter, eating breakfast with some coffee.

When the wood creaked under my feet she turned to me, "Good morning, Eleny."

"Good morning," I smiled as she offered me a muffin.

She filled another cup of coffee then handed it to me, "The others have already eaten and are getting ready to leave."

"Oh," I just remembered that I was leaving today and frowned.

"Want to eat out on the porch?" Raeya asked.

I nodded.

When we sat down in the rocking chairs, I was at a loss for words. Thankfully I had something sweet to occupy my mouth, otherwise I would have been biting my lip or fiddling with my fingers.

Finally Raeya broke the silence, "Eleny, don't look so glum, you will have a splendid time."

I tried a smile, but I think it turned out a weird grimace because then Raeya chortled, "Stop worrying, I won't be alone. And remember that no one was here when you came through that tunnel."

I nodded again, "I know, but it's not just that."

"What is it then?" Raeya said, her face twisting into a look of concern.

"I mean, it's hard to explain."

"I'm listening," she took a sip of her drink.

"To be honest, I think I'm scared of traveling with people I barely know. I mean, of course I am, who wouldn't? Also of where we're going to travel. There has to be dangers along the way."

"Elyon will protect you. He will protect you all."

"I know, I know. But I guess I am also nervous about meeting a girl my age. Polos was a small town, and there weren't many girls there. At all. All of the people my age were boys. So I just visited neighbors with my grandmother."

"Hmm," Raeya looked out to the forest then back at me, "I don't think that you need to worry so much, Teamalie has told me a lot about Perl. She seems like a very nice girl."

I nodded again as Grimblon Bend stepped up the stairs, "We're leaving now."

We stood and I hugged Raeya like never before. She sniffled and gazed down at me, "Go, and smell the rosemary along the way."

I smiled when she added the herb into the phrase. Taking a step back, I turned and followed Grimblon through the few trees to the entrance. The tunnel wasn't the one Noctua and I had come through, which was the front. We were going through the back.

Hopefully there aren't as many spiders.
"Yes, me hope so too. They disgusting."

Noctua landed on my shoulder as usual, then crawled around the back of my neck, through the hood of my cape, to my other shoulder.

Teamalie was already going through while Alex, with Deiless on his shoulder, was waiting for us.

I stepped through, the tunnel was wide enough for two Thasfaens to stand side by side, so

I walked next to Teamalie. The men followed, although Alex had to duck his head so he wouldn't hit the rock.

Biting back a laugh when I heard a *thunk* behind me, I linked my arm in Teamalie's.

She smiled, "You remind me of Perl," She said, patting my hand, "She loves to care for young ones, that's why she stayed with the other family. I miss her so, this is the first time that she's been away from us so long."

"Isn't it hard to travel without any other women?"

"Well, this is the first time I've traveled without Perl since she was born, so I can't say I'm used to it. But I have traveled with just me and Grimblon before, so it isn't the first time."

Smiling, I remembered how Grandmother would walk over to her friend's cottages and visit. How whenever she was shopping at the market, she would greet whoever came across her path. Tears came to my eyes again, it was like there was a hole in my heart with her gone.

Noctua shifted on my shoulder.

I was glad that there wasn't any more lighting, we'd gone far into the tunnel, because now the taste of salty tears were running down my face.

It's my fault that Grandmother is gone. Had I just gone into the tunnel like she urged, or had not gone with her and Palana at all, she would be at my side right now. But no. She isn't at my side. Teamalie is. It's my fault.

"It not your fault!" Noctua pecked at my head.

Ow! That hurt.

"Oops, me sorry. But it not your fault!"

You don't know, Noctua. You weren't there.

"But me felt what you felt, I see what happen!"

B-but you don't know what it actually f-feels like to lose the only mother you ever had!

I unlinked my arms from Teamalie's and got down on my hands and knees, the ceiling was getting lower, and followed. Noctua hopped down in front of me and spread her wings so she could block my path.

"But, me do!"

What do you mean? I stopped trying to get around her.

"Because," she looked down, "Because me lose my mother, too."

What?

"Few months before me left, Mother went hunting. And didn't come back." I sucked in a breath as she continued, "Father searched every day but couldn't find *even clue."* She gave a sad, quiet, whistle.

Oh, Noctua…

I smoothed her head feathers. She turned away.

Noctua… I'm sorry.

She turned back around and, unexpectedly, hopped up to me and touched her forehead against mine.

"It's alright, you not know." She turned back around and took off, the ceiling was starting to get higher as we crawled on. Eventually we could walk again, thankfully unlike the front entrance where you have to crawl almost the entire time.

When we finally saw light again I grinned.

Trekking down the mountain was treacherous, having to scoot up against the wall because the trail was so thin. All I could think was that Elyon was with me.

Now I was wishing we had gone the back way, considering the beautiful walk down. The wind was icy cold and it started to sprinkle.

Noctua was cuddled up on the back of my neck under the cape. out of the wind and rain. I reached back and smoothed her feathers when she got a little ruffled. At least she was keeping me warm.

    I heard someone shouting, but couldn't tell who, Grimblon was in front of me, Teamalie behind me, and Alex behind her. The rain picked up and the wind blew harder.

    I heard a shout again, and this time Grimblon turned around and walked past me to Alex. I stopped and turned around. They were talking about something, but I still couldn't hear. Then I had an idea.

    Noctua?

    She yawned and moved around so she could look out. *"Yes?"*

    Can you try to listen to the men? I can't hear.

    "Mm hmm." Her head poked out, flinching when the rain hit her feathers. She cocked her head left, then right. *"They say there is cave up ahead."*

    Thank You Elyon, I'm freezing!

    "Yes, men say we stop 'till storm leaves."

    Good.

    And sure enough, up ahead was a cave.

    Then the scream came from behind me.

    I gasped when I turned around.

    Rocks were falling down the cliff, one had bashed Teamalie's head and she was knocked out, laying on the ground.

Grimblon and Alex hoisted her quickly and we ran to the cave.

The entrance was quite small, but inside it opened up into a large cavern.

I got a blanket out and they laid her down on it. She was still unconscious, but breathing, and had a large, deep gash on her head.

"Teamalie? Teamalie, dear, can you hear me? Teamalie!" Grimblon cried out to her.

I didn't really want to tell them about my gift just yet, this way, but she wouldn't survive this with even all of my remedies.

"Grimblon, move. NOW." I said.

He looked up at me, tears streaming down his face. He scooted over and I knelt down, putting my hands on the bloody wound.

"Eleny, what are DOING?" Grimblon demanded.

"Shush, Grimblon. Look..." Alex pointed.

My hands started to glow dimly, then lightened up as bright as a fire. I sat there, after a minute closing my eyes.

It was like time stopped.

Something touched my arm.

"Eleny?"

I opened my eyes, Teamalie's eyes were open, too, her hand was resting on my arm.

"Teamalie!" Grimblon embraced and kissed her. "Oh thank Elyon! You're alright!"

I backed up to give them space, my eyes about to close from the wave of sleepiness. It took a lot of energy to heal a person.

Alex came and sat in front of me, his face solemn. "You have a gift. The healing gift. That's why you were learning about herbs."

I nodded and stood, barely able to get off the ground.

I started to lose balance, and the floor started spinning as I fell, but Alex caught me by the waist, "That obviously took much of your strength."

"I'm fine, I'm fine. Just help me up," I tried to stand again, but it ended in the same result.

"Eleny! Are you alright?" Alex held me tighter to keep me steady, "Where's your folding box?"

I muttered, my eyes closing, "Cape pocket."

He set me down and grabbed my cape from the floor and took out the box.

I didn't know what happened next,

everything went dark.

All I knew was that I woke up near a fire and Alex was laying down on his mat not far away from mine. Noctua was curled up in my cape, near my pillow. Grimblon and Teamalie were under their covers, on the other side of the fire.

I rubbed my eyes, yawned, and stood up.

The floor made my feet shiver through my boots, then I realized my boots weren't on, only my stockings. My boots were at the end of my mat.

I guess I'll start getting things out now.

"You do that, me stay here." Noctua cuddled back into my hood after coming out to look around.

I decided to change out of my clothes. So I got dressed into my white blouse and brown breaches, then my socks, in the closet.

Then I took out my box, having another idea.

Please work, please work, please work.

I whispered into it, "Separate into three boxes."

I watched it open up all the way, then it kept opening until it was three times bigger than the original size! I gasped, it stopped for a second, then separated into three. When it was done separating, they folded back into small boxes.

I turned around to see that everyone stared at me.

"Uh," I smiled and picked them up, then handed one to Alex, my hands shivering when his fingers brushed mine, and one to the Bends, they all had questioning looks. "I had an idea and tried it out," I gestured to the boxes in their hands, "and it worked! These are for you."

Teamalie looked at me and smiled, "Thank you, Eleny, but not for the box," she stood and walked over to me, "but for saving me." She gave me a hug, and I squeezed back.

"I explained to them last night what you did," Alex came over.

Grimblon grunted, "Yes, and I apologize for shouting at you. I was very distressed. We do not deserve this gift from you, more like you deserve something from us."

I shook my head, "No apology needed, although I appreciate it. I was never angry at you. Although I do have one request."

"You name it, dear." Teamalie looked at me.

My face grew serious and I stared down at

my lap, "Don't tell anyone what I did."

Grimblon and Teamalie frowned, "If that's what you want. But are you sure you want to give this folding box to us?"

"Of course! These are gifts for you, for being so kind to me and letting me travel with you."

They all beamed as I showed them how to open up the boxes and where to put things. They all put their things in it, thanking me a whole lot more than need be. Then they got dressed in their closets like I did.

After everyone was done I sat on my pallet, eating a biscuit. Noctua was eating a piece of meat that I packed for her on my cape.

Alex closed his box up and sat next to me on my mat, "Are you sure you're alright and will be able to travel today?"

I nodded, "I should be fine. The last time this happened I slept until the next morning and was fine the rest of the day."

He nodded, then cocked his head, "I'm confused about something."

My legs shivered at how close he was, "What?"

He frowned, "Why didn't you tell me you

had a gift?"

I looked at the fire, "I don't know. I had already told everyone so much, this was a little more private to me." I looked back at his face, "In Patera they would kill me if they knew. I've seen it happen."

His eyes softened and he touched my arm, "But you're not in Patera anymore, you're with us. Out here. Elyon will protect you. And it isn't against the law in the Plains."

I swallowed, "I know." I stood and brushed my arm where he touched it. "I'm going to start getting ready to leave, so up."

He got off my mat and I rolled it up as he did the same to his.

THIRTEEN

Attacked

We were soon off again! When everything was packed up we went out of the cave. We started walking down the mountain again.

Now that I could see, the view was breathtaking. We were already more than half way down, but you could still see out over the fields. The Way River was in sight, but the other mountains were blocking the fields near Wix Town.

I sighed, we had a long way to go.

Maybe we could ride the wixes the rest of the way there. But that would be too much work for them.

"Yes, carrying two people that far would be very hard. We have to take many stops." Noctua flew overhead, then landed on my shoulder.

I thought of last night. After I passed out Alex must have made up my mat and laid me down on it. I blushed at the thought of him picking me up. Then I thought of how he touched my arm this morning.

Oh shut up brain, what's wrong with you? It's not like Grimblon and Teamalie could have moved me, Teamalie was still a little weak, and Grimblon was with her.

I distracted myself by trying to figure out a way to get to Wix Town faster, before the snow blew in.

Noctua tapped my shoulder with her foot. She gestured down the path, I hadn't realized that Teamalie was trying to get my attention.

"What?" I shouted, they were a ways in front of me.

I must have been daydreaming, looking out at the view.

"You were."

I can see that.

"Eleny, come! We see a wagon down at the base of the mountain!" Teamalie shouted back.

Jogging to them, I looked down, and there was a wagon. When I caught up to where they were waiting, I noticed Teamalie looked less worn out without her pack weighing her down.

Alex told me their plan, "It's up to you, Eleny. We think we can catch up to the wagon if we fly the wixes down. Two people at a time."

"Just wait a second, won't that be too difficult for the wixes?"

"Deiless is fine, it's up to Noctua."

I nodded, "Let me ask her."

Noctua?

"Yes?"

Do you think you could fly two people down to that wagon? I pointed.

"Oh, yes. That easy."

"She says yes. So of course!" I replied, "Especially if we can get there sooner."

Grimblon grinned at that, "Then let's get going already."

Alex spoke, "And I'll call Deiless, he went out for a flight."

Okay Noctua. Time to turn into wix form.

Her talons moved around lightly, not to

pierce through the fabric. She took off flawlessly into the air, hovering for a few seconds, then landed on a small boulder.

"We go now? We go now?"

I grinned and stifled a laugh at how insistent and energetic she was. *Just wait a second, let me ask them something first.*

I turned to Grimblon, "Who's riding with me?"

"Teamalie. Deiless will be able to carry two men, I'm not sure Noctua would be able to so I'm riding with Alex."

Teamalie then walked over, "This will be fun."

Alright Noctua-

But she was already in wix form by the time I turned back around. She bent down and I sat on her, Teamalie following.

Good idea, Noctua, for crouching down so Teamalie could get on with ease.

"I remember when you had hard time getting on me. You got hurt. I not want that for this kind woman, but I guess it was funny watching you run into my side."

"Teamalie, you might want to tuck in your dress as much as possible."

She nodded at me and when settled, she

said, "Oh, this makes me miss Melodia even more."

Curious, I asked, "Who's Melodia?"

"She's my wix."

"You have a wix! Why wouldn't she be here with you? Where in the world is she?" I asked as Noctua took off.

"She, and Grimblon's wix, Corvus, are back with Perl! We didn't want to leave Perl all alone, so they're watching over her!" she called, while Noctua did a short dive.

"You *both* have wixes?" I asked, shocked that no one had told me.

"Yes."

Noctua glided gracefully the rest of the way down, landing without a jolt a few yards in front of the wagon. I glanced at the man holding the reins, his mouth was agape as he stopped the horse.

Noctua stepped a bit closer, and that was when I realized that the man was huge! And the horses were more than two times the normal size of a horse, which was much taller than Noctua.

There was a light tap on my shoulder, Teamalie smiled at me, "Don't you think we should get down and greet the poor man?"

Embarrassed, I bit my lip and got down,

then followed Teamalie as she went to the stranger, Noctua walking behind me.

"Hello!" Teamalie hollered to the man, "Sorry we frightened you."

The man seemed to break out of his daze, "Oh, um, no need to be sorry," he examined us for a second, "I just did not expect two women and a wix to drop down out of nowhere."

As the Jinde finished his sentence Alex dropped down behind us with a thud. I stepped back and let them explain that we needed a ride to Wix Town. The man's name was Zepho Mikkun.

The Jinde had a bushy black beard, curly hair that was graying, and wore an elk skin tunic. Zepho said that he lived in River Port, and Wix Town was on the way there. He came here to hunt for his family for a week a few times a year and now he was going home.

I grinned when he agreed to let us ride to our destination. Noctua had already turned back into barn owl form at the beginning of the conversation and was perched on my shoulder. I could tell that she was tired from the short flight down, and carrying more than one person for the first time must have been exhausting.

Zepho jumped down off of the enormous

covered wagon and turned to show us where we could sit in the back. Now that he was on ground level I saw how tall he really was. He dwarfed Grimblon, who was tall for a Thasfaen, like a hound to a hare. He was even taller than Alex, who was at least six feet, where I'm at four feet.

Zepho helped us into the wagon by setting up a chair for us to step up onto to climb in. Alex went first, then Grimblon helped his wife up. When Grimblon struggled but finally was in, I climbed up the old chair.

I reached to pull myself up, but there was nothing to grab onto for leverage.

After trying to pull myself up more than a few times, I saw Alex come, "Need some help?"

I blushed then decided to go with sarcasm, "Oh, no. I just love the view from here. I think I'll stay with my arms resting like this while we travel."

He rolled his eyes and held out his hand, "Come here."

I hesitated, but grabbed it. His warm hands pulled me up onto the wagon floor. When I had my footing I let go of him as soon as possible.

I looked around, the others were leaning against the side and were already asleep.

They must not have slept well like I did.

"I don't think so." Noctua landed down on the floor.

Frowning, I brought out the blankets and covered them up, then cuddled up in a blanket of my own, realizing Alex had been watching me.

I tried and tried to sleep, but the bumpiness of the ride was too rough to relax and not stay tense. Finally I decided, stepping around every one who were now all asleep, to go sit with Zepho at the front.

I poked my head out and welcomed the breeze, he was whipping the reins. Gathering up my courage, I tapped his shoulder lightly.

He took notice of me and glanced back, "You want to sit up here gal?"

"Yes, thanks," I mumbled, stepping around him to sit on the seat, "The others are asleep, but it was too bumpy for me to rest."

"Same here," Alex poked his head out and plunked down beside me.

"Well, you're both welcome to be here," he nodded then gave a hint of a smile, "I don't get company very often when I travel, so this is a treat. What's your name, Thasfaen?"

"Eleny Nil."

My cheeks heated when he nodded and said, "Pretty name, for a pretty little maiden. And what about you, Xelman?"

"Alexovin, sir."

"A fine name."

I was squished between Alex and the side of the seat. My legs started to have goose bumps by how close he was, so I distracted myself again, this time by the scenery.

It was exquisite. The trees, aspen, cedar, and some that I couldn't name, were on both sides of the trail. The aspen's leaves were yellow, and the trees I didn't know were all shades of reds and oranges. But an icy wind, cutting right through the cape wrapped around me, was a reminder that the cold season was coming. We had to get out of the mountains before it started to snow.

Gathering my voice I asked, "What are those trees with the oranges and reds?"

"Oh, those are maple trees," Alex replied.

"They are very pretty."

"Yes. I agree."

The wagon hit a rock in the road, making it bump up. Before I knew what was happening, I realized I landed on Alex when it did.

Leaning on his chest, my heart beat quickly

as heat climbed up my neck.

"Why hello there," Alex said, grinning down at me.

Then the heat reached my face as he lifted me by the waist and slid me back to my seat.

I quickly looked back at the foliage, thinking of how his muscles were thick and strong as he had picked me up easily.

Go away stupid thoughts!

Hey Noctua, you should see these beautiful trees.

She came out of my hood and sat in my lap, staring at the foliage. *"We used live in place with colorful trees like these."*

You mean you and your parents?

"Yeah." her voice cracked.

I wanted to pull her into an embrace, but knowing she probably wouldn't like it, I just smoothed her head feathers.

We sat silently until the others woke up a few hours later. We were at the foot of the mountain now, the sun about to set behind it.

When we stopped near a river, I jumped down and took my dirty clothes from my box to the water. I scrubbed my white blouse until all of the dark spots were out. Then did the same to my breeches. Teamalie followed and did the same, except she did the men's clothes too.

"Ugh, I don't think I would clean those shirts in a thousand years!" I said, disgusted.

Teamalie just chuckled, "Oh Eleny, I've been doing it since we began traveling years ago."

Disgusted even more, I hung my garments up, on a string that we attached from one tree to another, to dry. I was glad it was a ways away from the camp, for my undergarments were hanging, too.

Then we, including Zepho, had the lettuce, cheese, and herb dressing sandwiches, that I had packed, around the fire. I sat on my blanket, the Bends on there's too. Zepho was sitting on the end of his covered wagon and Alex was on a tree stump near me.

Noctua went hunting then came back with a full stomach. I laughed right out, the others joining me, when she kept making moaning sounds from being so stuffed.

"It not funny, I shouldn't have tried to eat that enormous rat. It was as big as Deiless."

I giggled again.

"Alex Hendruton to Eleny Nil."

I glanced, eyes round, at the Xelman, he was looking out into the woods. *Uh, welcome.*

"There's something out there."

Huh?

His voice was grave. I stared out into the darkness where he was looking. The moon wasn't out, and the stars were covered by the trees. The only way I could see Alex was for the fire.

"There's something out there."

I don't see anything.

"What about your wix?"

Oh, duh. I looked at Noctua. *Can you look out there and see what is bothering Alex?*

She stood up and looked out into the darkness, cocking her head left, then right.

What do you see?

She turned her head to me, her black eyes as big as I'd ever seen them. *"Something very bad."*

The darkness over came me. I stood and stepped into the forest a few feet. No one noticed.

I peered deeper and saw five dark shadows lurking.

I stepped one more step.

Then everything around me became a blur.

Without warning, the most hideous black thing ran towards me with lightning speed, lashing out with it's long talons.

I fell backwards and it clawed at my arm as

I screamed.

Then Alex was there, he sliced the monster to bits.

Blackness took over.

I heard voices, people surrounded me.

"Eleny!" "Is she awake?" "Oh, that looks really bad!"

I opened my eyes, "W-what happened?"

Alex's face came into a blurry view, "A Morden attacked you and as I killed it you lost consciousness."

I winced as pain came to my arm, I looked down and gasped, "Oh, man. That hurts really bad."

Teamalie was beside me, sitting me up. "Oh... I've never treated something this horrid!" She covered her face.

Blood started pouring out of my arm as I groaned and took out my box, handing it to Teamalie. "Open it up and get my bandages. Hurry, before I lose too much blood!"

She took the box and opened it.

I asked her, "Have you ever sewn a blanket before?"

She nodded anxiously.

"Then you might want to help me because I don't think I can do it with one hand." I groaned again, the pain was blinding, making my surroundings spin.

Alex's voice came to me, it was soft and gentle, but urgency was behind it. *"Eleny, no. You need to stay awake. Don't. Fall. Asleep. Focus on my voice. Say Elyon imi kudoz."*

Elyon imi kudoz.

The warmth came, but my arm was still screaming.

Teamalie took out my special needle and thread, then looked back at me, "What next?"

"Have you ever sewed up a ripped cloth?"

"Yes, many!"

"Then do that to my arm!"

I closed my eyes and grimaced as she stuck the needle in.

After she was done I instructed her to use the basil and sage salve. It stung as she applied the medicine, but I knew that it would keep out infection. After she made sure the bandages covered the whole wound, I noticed that Noctua was flying in the air, whistling down at me, worried.

I'll be alright Noctua, come down here.

She glided down and landed in my lap, burying her head in my blouse. Then I realized Alex was staring at me with wide, scared eyes.

After Teamalie helped me put the items back she went over to her husband, then Alex came up and knelt down next to me. "Sorry I couldn't stay by you while Teamalie was stitching you up, I couldn't watch." His face was paler than usual, "Are you alright?"

I nodded, gave a weak smile, and jested, "Nice that you're thinkin' of me."

He frowned. "I'm so sorry, Eleny. This is my fault. I shouldn't have asked you what was out there."

His light green eyes were sincere and a worry line appeared between his eyebrows. I suddenly had an urge to make it disappear and smooth it out, but restrained my hands.

Instead I just went with this to lighten the mood. "It's fine Alex. You were just worried. I'm not dead." I rolled my eyes.

He didn't smile back, "I'm still really sorry."

I could tell it would help if I said this, "I forgive you, there's nothing more to say."

He looked relieved and the worry line disappeared for half a second, but then he frowned again, "What did Noctua see?"

I then frowned back, "There are more Mordens, Alex, at least five of them."

His face turned from concern to alarm, "What?"

I took a shaky breath, "They saw me when I came closer, that's when everything happened."

"We need to be ready then!" he stood and walked to Zepho, "Get your weapon, Mordens will be here soon." Then looked at Teamalie, "Help her into the wagon, you two will sleep there tonight."

I jumped up, regretting it, "Yowch!" I cradled my arm.

"You need to take it easy, young lady," Teamalie said, picking up my blanket that was on the ground for me.

"Thank you, Teamalie."

She nodded and headed to the wagon. Zepho helped us get in. When we were settled I peeked out, the men were getting their weapons ready.

But something was missing.

Wait, where's Noctua?

FOURTEEN

Recovering and Continuing

Teamalie and I searched for Noctua in the covered wagon, but she was nowhere to be seen.

Noctua? Noctua!

"Me outside of wagon in a tree, I far from evil creatures."

Oh, thank Elyon you're alright!

I relayed the news to Teamalie, and she looked relieved.

Noctua came and landed on the edge. I gave her a little hug, then sat back as she cuddled up in my lap.

I was so worried something had happened to you when you were outside.

"Me know, and me sorry."

It's alright, I'm just glad you're safe.

"Me thought you were gonna die!"

Who, me? Never. I'll always be here for you.

She gave her sad whistle, even though muffled. *"Me mother say that too, but she gone now."*

I didn't know what to say to that.

I peeked out again.

Alex was sitting on the tree stump, then pulled out the slim sword from his cape. I wondered about that. Where did he learn to use it? In fact, where did he get it? I decided to ask him later.

The wind picked up, turning colder. A rustling came from the bushes, the men stood up tensely.

Elyon be with them.

The bush rustled for a moment more and then stopped. I let out a sigh of relief, maybe they would leave us alone. But just as the thought crossed my mind, the next ugliest thing I had ever seen leaped out of the bushes. With the Morden's teeth bared, it growled and circled around the men. I gasped as it lashed out at Zepho, but he shot an arrow between the eyes. I looked away, I couldn't bear seeing the picture.

Then I heard another low growl. Glancing back out I saw a Morden jump from the trees, another following close behind, and charged toward the men.

Turning, I noticed Teamalie's closed eyes as she mumbled a prayer. Noctua was watching the fight, there were shouts and the sound of shooting arrows.

Then it went quiet.

Noctua hopped over to me. *"It safe, I fly out."*
Are you sure?

She cocked her head to listen, then turned it back to me and nodded.

Fine, just please be careful.

She took off and I stood up, the men were surrounded by a few bodies.

Alex glanced up at me, "Stay in there for now, they're gone, but we don't know if they will come back, even if their leader is dead."

I gulped and sat back down, eventually falling asleep.

Something moved by me. Opening my

eyes, I saw that Noctua was changing position in the blankets. It looked like the sun was about to be up so I hopped down out of the wagon to walk to the stream. All of the men were sleeping by the fire.

I winced as my arm jolted.

After I was refreshed, having to use only one hand to wash my face, I checked on my clothes that were hanging up. They were there, unexpectedly. I was worried the Mordens would've gotten hold of them. They were dry so I started putting them in my box.

I heard a rustle nearby and jumped, turning towards the noise.   Alex was coming from up the river, heading back to the camp.

I let out a breath as he passed by, "Phew, you scared me for a minute."

He grinned, "Sorry." Then his eyes got big, his face became tinted red, and he cleared his throat, "Well, um, I'll see you back at the camp," He walked away quickly.

Huh, that was weird, why did he walk away so fast? Then I looked down and saw that I was holding one of my undergarments. Heat coming to my face, I stuffed it into my box like the speed of lightning.

The sun was coming up now, so I went back to the camp.

Teamalie was making coffee over the fire with the pot that used to hang on Grimblon's pack. I was glad that I gave them that box, it would serve them well.

I sat next to her, noticing that the men, thankfully, must have moved the Morden bodies elsewhere the night before. Noctua flew out of the covered wagon and landed on the stump beside me.

"Me going to hunt, me come right back."

Alright, but be careful. Tell us if you see anything that might mean Mordens could be near.

"Okay, me will."

She flew out into the pale orange and yellow forest.

Teamalie looked at my arm, "Is it okay, dear?"

I grimaced and looked down, "I won't die from the pain."

She nodded and went back to poking the fire with her stick.

Soon the other men arose, waking just when the breakfast, sweet oat bread with a side of coffee, was finished.

After we ate, I noticed Grimblon, Alex, and even Zepho, had cuts that were covered with dry blood on their arms and legs.

"It must have been a pretty bad fight last night, huh?" I said.

They all stared at me, except for Alex, who was still a little red and was averting his eyes.

Wanting to do what I had trained for, I opened my box up to get my bandages and chamomile and basil salves that were in jars. Teamalie came to help too. I was more thankful than she could have ever known. To be honest, the pain might *have* just killed me if I let it. It was really hard to clean wounds and wrap them one handed.

All of them resisted, but when Teamalie gave both Grimblon and Alex stern looks that said *'You're going to get it and that's final,'* they finally clamped their mouths shut and quit protesting.

Teamalie and I first washed the cuts with rags that we dipped in the stream, assuming it was clean water. Then we dipped other clean rags into the chamomile salve then slathered it on the cuts. The men didn't complain when it stung, which I admired. When I put on a basil salve to relieve pain, they thanked me. When we were done, I put the strips of cloth on the wounds.

I held Alex's hand while I wrapped it. He had a large cut on the back of it.

"Thank you," he whispered, looking at me when I finished.

Heat climbed up my neck and I dropped his hand quickly, then I smirked, "Now we're even, sort of. You saved me, I save your hand from infection and pain."

He grinned back.

The heat came again.

What is WRONG with me?!

I turned away quickly and got in the wagon and we continued our journey.

I sat up front, thankfully away from Alex, who decided to sit back there this time, because I had NO idea what happened a while ago.

Noctua was standing in my lap as Zepho told me about his family. He had three grandchildren, two boys and a girl. He also had a farm, with many kinds of animals that his grandchildren loved to play with. We all laughed with him when he told stories.

Eventually we were out in the bare, open, fields and saw a farm house every now and then. The sun was high in the sky. Noctua and Deiless were racing back and forth, above and around the wagon.

"When will we get there?" I asked.

"Oh," said the Jinde, "around noon tomorrow."

I sighed glumly, "I think I'll go and rest in the back for a while." I stood up and crawled around him to get to the back. It was cold and dusty.

"We'll stop for a break at the river, I need to let the horse rest," Zepho called.

I jumped down on the floor, Teamalie was gazing out of the wagon, Alex was leaning up against the side, reading a book, and Grimblon was heading to the front.

Probably going to discuss something with Zepho.

I brought out a blanket and laid down in front of Teamalie. I couldn't fall asleep, so I got lost in thought.

After a while the wagon jolted. I sat up and peered at the front, Zepho had gotten down and was probably unhitching the horse to lead to the water.

I stood up and jumped out of the wagon, surveying the area. There were oak trees surrounding us and you could see the Way River down a trail.

When Zepho came back, I sighed again. Getting down, I opened up my box so I could get the chairs and table to have lunch. Teamalie helped me set up and we all had food together in the small bunch of trees.

We then continued on for the rest of the day.

When I shifted under the blanket, an icy breeze shot through the opening I made when moving. I groaned and sat up, everyone was still asleep, and the fire in the center of our circle of blankets was out. Noctua was still under my blanket, moving around, stuck. *"Can't you help me out?"*

I stifled a laugh then flipped the cloth back so she could get out. Her voice popped up in my head again. *"Now me regret coming out, it's so cold!"*

She snuggled up against me and I covered her back up. I then stood up, holding the buff colored bird, and went closer to the pit to start the fire back up. When it was aglow, I sat on the mossy ground and warmed my hands. Noctua came back out of the little cocoon she made to sit in my lap.

"You're an early riser, huh?"

I glanced up as Alex sat across from me and scooted closer to the fire to warm his hands.

I nodded and then whispered, "I wasn't really before I left, I normally stayed up late." I bit my lip, "But now that I've been so tired by the end of the day, I go to sleep earlier."

When he stayed silent I remembered that I hadn't been able to ask him about something. "I saw that you had a sword, where'd you learn to use it?"

He turned his gaze to me, "My grandfather, the one I inherited mindvoicing from," but didn't give anything else.

Knowing I probably wouldn't get any more information, my lips pressed together.

Noctua yawned and stood up. *"Me going to hunt."*

Okay, be sure to come back before we leave.

She took off and flew through the trees. I watched after her until her golden wings were out of sight.

Alex got my attention, "Why don't you just heal yourself?"

I frowned, "I don't think I can. I bestow

peace upon another, that's how I heal the person."

"You can at least try."

I closed my eyes, trying to feel the peace. It didn't come. "Nope."

He nodded and stared at the fire.

"Alex?"

He turned his head to me, "What?"

I took a breath and blurted, "I want to know how to defend myself with a weapon." Before he said anything I continued, "I just hate being vulnerable. Yes, I have Noctua, but what if she gets injured?" I said, thinking of Jone. "I mean, on the way to Raeya's, I didn't have Noctua at first. I was so nervous about bandits, or the men from the raid, for that matter. Another example is last night," I gestured to my arm, "Please, Alex. Even if how short I am is a disadvantage, I should be able to learn how to defend myself somehow."

He looked me up and down, "Well, I think you're perfect just the way you-" His eyes grew and his cheeks darkened, as if he didn't mean to say that out loud. "I, I mean actually, your height would be an *advantage*, come to think of it." He stuck his hand in the pocket of his tree bark colored cape, pulling out his box. He whispered something into it, then pulled out a blade. It wasn't a short sword nor a dagger. "This is something I picked up in Whim. You can get one for yourself once we reach River Port. It's called an Ynit, it's meant for Thasfaens like you." He handed it to me, hilt pointed at my chest.

I reached over the fire and grabbed it.

It wasn't as heavy as it seemed, I swiped it slowly a few times back and forth. The thin point glistened. The silver reflected of the fire, making it glow in my hand.

I heard Alex chuckle and glanced up, heat rising up my neck again. "What?" *More like 'what is wrong with me?'.*

He shook his head and smothered the smile, "Nothing." Then he stood, myself following, and pulled his sword out of it's sheath. "Like I said, your height would be an advantage. In a battle, you need to be quick and light on your feet. Since you are shorter," He blushed again, "no offense-"

"None taken."

"-You need to aim for the legs, you won't be able to reach your opponent's chest or head, unless you are fighting another Thasfaen. You could aim for the feet, but most likely your opponent will be wearing shoes and it's best just to aim for the legs or lower torso. Don't aim for the knees unless you're behind the person, then you could strike forward with the tip of the blade."

I nodded, absorbing all he said.

"If your opponent wears armor, there are few maneuvers to get through it. By then you just need to learn when you can't win a fight. If it's just a sword and shield then you still just need to focus on the feet, unless you can get around to behind him, then strike."

I nodded again as he came around the fire.

"The Ynit has a different technique than a long or short sword, it involves rolls, flips, and spins. You can throw it, but it isn't easy. Unless, of course, you're a Jinde, it's the size of a dagger to them." He held up his sword.

I followed suit.

He huffed a laugh, "Don't start quite yet, we're not going fight, I'll just show you the common positions people use." He lifted the tip of his blade as high as his head, hands as low as his waist.

He swiped left swift and hard, then swiped right, then he lifted it and struck down, then swiped back up.

He took a step back, "You won't be doing these maneuvers. These are for swordsman. You will be learning the Ynit. Before we begin with the Ynit, I will ask Grimblon to teach you how to flip and roll. Keep the Ynit by your side for now." He sheathed his sword and walked swiftly away.

    Soon everyone was up and around, we ate breakfast, and then got back into the covered wagon. Since it was so cold this morning, Zepho closed up the cover all the way so we were snug. But both the wixes were restless, so we let them out to race outside, while we stayed thankfully warm.

    Every now and then I peeked outside through the front, but not much of the scenery had changed. Just oak trees with the occasional elm. As the day wore on, it got warmer and warmer, and eventually we had to open the cover back up. I shed my blanket and put it away, then sat at the front with Zepho and Alex again, this time Zepho between us.

    By noon we had come to the outskirts of Wix Town.

    Boy, and everywhere you looked someone had a wix in bird form on their shoulder or flying close behind them. Or in wix form flying over head or trailing behind its bonded while they went to a neighbor's.

When we passed the big houses and little cottages, we came into the center of town, where the shops and inns were. We stopped at the town stables and Zepho led the horses into it.

While the men went into the large barn, Teamalie and I walked into town, Noctua on the shoulder opposite from my bad arm.

The town was very busy, people shouted, horses trotted through the streets, but the loudest noise of all was the calls, tweets, peeps, caws, and screeches of birds. The wixes were in bird form more here than the outskirts of Wix Town. No wonder that's what they called it.

"Oh Eleny, me never see so many wixes at one time in my entire life!"

I stifled a laugh as she eagerly watched, and probably talked to the other wixes.

Teamalie linked her arm in my healthy one, something we had been doing quite often, when I said, "I saw a clothes shop I wanted to stop at. I need a new blouse and breeches, my old ones are starting to fall apart."

"I'll stop by with you, Eleny, I need some new stockings."

I smiled, Teamalie was becoming more than

a friend, she was becoming more like a motherly figure to me.

I saw the shop and pointed it out. We went inside and bought what we needed. I used some of the money Jone had given me before I left. I chose a dark chocolate brown blouse and and some black breeches.

When we came back out, I heard a loud gasp.

I searched around and saw her.

A Thasfaen girl, about my age, was running toward us.

She had Teamalie's reddish auburn colored hair, and Grimblon's big, dark, sapphire blue eyes.

Perl.

FIFTEEN

Water fun

Mother , Mother! Oh Mother!"

I stepped back and bit my lip as the mother and daughter embraced.

"Mother, I missed you so much!"

"And I you!" Teamalie squeezed tighter then stepped back, gesturing to me, "This is Eleny, she's been traveling with us."

I gave a little smile and a shy wave.

The girl came up to me, she had a few

freckles sprinkled on her face, was wearing riding clothes, which was strange for me to see another girl wearing, and she grinned from ear to ear, "Hello Eleny. My name's Perlelia, but you probably already knew that."

She held her hand out to me, I took it with my good one and she shook hardily.

I grinned back, "I've heard a lot about you."

She giggled then looked at her mother, then her voice turned serious, "The house was a wreck when we got here, something got in, a raccoon or something else, and made itself at home," she sighed, "We cleaned it up for the entire day and well into the afternoon the next day, but now it's livable."

Her mother sighed, too, "Well, we'll only be here for about a week more, then we'll go on."

Perl nodded.

"Wait, you live here?" I asked, eyebrows raised.

Teamalie chuckled, "Yes, the house we mentioned is ours."

"I guess no one told me."

"How about we go there now?"

"Sounds good to me, I think I need to rest my arms, the one holding it up is starting to get tired."

Teamalie nodded then started to head down the walk way and we followed. When we started to cross the street Teamalie looked to Perl, "How is Temmen?" she said, seeming to lift Perl's spirit.

"He's doing just fine." She giggled again, "and he's started to crawl, so you can imagine how naughty he's been."

"Is Temmen a little one you've been helping take care of?" I asked, when we reached the other side of the street.

"Yes, and his big brother, Amalek, and sister Tsuli, who are three and five."

"I bet it takes a lot of patience."

"A lot and more," she grimaced, then she changed the subject, "You'll have to stay with me in my room!" she said happily, "I have some big quilts that we can make into a pallet, and you're going to love looking out the window into the garden!" She kept on telling me about her room until I noticed two birds flying behind us and one on her shoulder.

I looked up at Noctua, she was on my shoulder and was looking around excitedly. Then I looked back at Perl, she had stopped talking and was gawking at Noctua, apparently just noticing her. I saw Teamalie walk into the house so I sat on the porch steps, Perl sitting down, too. The sun was high in the sky, and now I was sweating.

Where in the world did the cold this morning go?

Perl turned her wide, blue, eyes at me, "Is it a wix?"

She pulled me out of my daze, "Uh, yes, *she* is a barn owl wix, her name is Noctua," I smiled.

Noctua stared back at Perl as she said, "She's so very pretty. Out of all of the wixes I've seen, which that's many, I've never seen a barn owl wix."

"Are those three over there," I pointed to some birds in a sapling, "Your wixes?"

"Yeah, just wait a second," she looked at them and they came flying to her, then landed on her arms.

"This one," she gestured to a bird with a white head that faded into a salmon pink under it's black wings. It's black tail was three times longer than its body, and it was split in two, like scissors for cutting fabric. The bird flew up onto Perl's shoulder and affectionately rubbed up against her neck.

Perl continued, "This one is a scissor-tail

wix, she's mine, and her name is Timna. This one is Melodia, my mother's song sparrow wix, and this one, a hooded crow wix, who's my father's, is Corvus."

The one she called Melodia was so small that she could fit in the palm of my hand. She had two brown stripes on her head, and one that went from her eye to the back of her head like a crown. Her beak was gray, and her wings were striped blacks and browns. Her breast was white, and had a few brown streaks, a thicker one in the center. I couldn't imagine what she looked like when she was in wix form.

Corvus was the same height of Noctua, but his tale was longer. He was only two colors, his head was black, and so was his throat, wings, and beak, and the rest of him was a light gray. His beak was a shiny onyx, thick and sleek.

Perl stood up, "Father and Mother left them with me." she looked at the people walking by, "I do have to say, even if I was a little reluctant, wanting to do this without babysitters, I was secretly relieved. It also helped me not miss my parents so much." She turned and grinned her huge grin at me, "You want to come and see my room?"

"Sure."

Perl walked through the front door and I followed. We entered a sitting room, with a sofa and cushioned chairs. Then she went through another door, and I followed her through a hallway.

An open door revealed a kitchen, with Teamalie inside at the sink. She was now wearing riding clothes, too. She turned around and saw me, "Oh, Eleny, we're having lunch in a little bit," then Melodia flew in and landed on her finger, "Oh, Melodia!" she exclaimed, smiling. She looked back at me, "Don't forget."

I sighed, "Oh I won't, my stomach won't let me forget, I'm starving."

She laughed as I followed Perl to another door. She opened it, and I saw a quaint and clean room. The walls were yellow, her bedspread a pale pink. A window was open, and you could see, as Perl had said, a flower garden with wooden bird feeders.

Perl walked up behind me, Timna on her head, as I leaned on the sil, letting my arms rest.

"Ooh, it pretty."

I glanced at Noctua. *Yes it is.*

Perl looked down into the garden with me, "I put bird feeders there for the seed eating wixes last week, that's how long we've been here waiting for my parents and Alex. When the wixes come and eat it, Timna, Melodia, and Corvus go down to visit with them."

I nodded and turned back to the room, there was a bed on one wall, a wardrobe and dresser with a mirror on the other. Noctua hopped off and glided gracefully to land on the back of the only chair in the room.

Perl sat on her bed, "What happened to your arm?"

I grimaced, reliving the memory.

"Sorry, that was probably rude of me."

I turned to the frowning Perl, "Mordens attacked us a few days ago."

"Oh my, that's not good." She paused. "Does it hurt?"

"Of course!" Realizing that sounded rude, I winced and said, "Sorry. I think the pain and having to hold it up with my other arm is getting to me."

"Oh, don't worry. It would to me too."

Another pause.

"Hey, I have an idea, be right back!" Perl darted out the door and came back a minute later with a long piece of fabric. "You can sling your arm with this, here let me help."

She tied the fabric around my shoulder and laid my arm gently in it.

"Thanks," I smiled.

"Don't mention it, glad I could help! Oh, do you want to set up your bed right now?"

Teamalie's voice echoed through the house, "Girls!"

I glanced at Perl, "Let's just do it tonight," I said, heading to the door.

She nodded and jumped up off the bed. Perl, with Noctua and Timna, were close behind me as I headed through the hall.

Teamalie was in the hall with a basket in the crook of her arm. "We're going to have a picnic," the ends of her lips turned up a little bit, "Zepho is going to drive us there."

"Who's Zepho?" Perl asked, as we followed her mother through the house to the front.

I pointed to the man in the covered wagon on the road in front of us, "Him. He gave us a ride, had he not we wouldn't have gotten here until next week."

"Ah."

I stepped up to the Jinde in the seat, "Hello."

He took notice of me, "Why hello, Eleny, are you feeling any better?"

"Much better, thank you. I hear we're going to have a picnic, where are we going?" I had gotten comfortable around him, so it wasn't that hard for me to ask questions anymore like it used to.

He gave a mischievous grin and winked, "You'll see."

Not wanting to leave Perl out, I sat in the back with her, Teamalie, Alex, and Grimblon instead of up front with Zepho. The wagon soon started rolling and bumping.

Curious, I asked, "Where's the other family you talked about?"

Perl answered me, "They're on an outing themselves, just them and the children. They should be here when we get back."

I yawned as Noctua cuddled up in my lap.

I glanced up to see Perl yawn, too, then she grinned, "Ha ha! It's contagious!"

Alex rolled his eyes, but smiled anyways.

Soon the wagon jolted, I searched the front and saw Zepho jump down. Everyone got out.

"There's a pool here that the river flows into," Zepho said, feeding the horse.

"I think I'll go cool off for a little bit then," I said.

Shielding my eyes, I followed Teamalie down to the little beach. I then sat on a stone and dipped my hot feet into the cool, clear, water. The sun was beating down on us. Noctua came and landed on my shoulder.

This must be one of the last warm days before the cold comes. Want to join me?

"Me guess, but I going to be in wix form."

She flew off and turned into her elegant wix self. She started to head back up the trail.

Hey, I thought that you were going to stay here!

But then she turned around and ran straight towards me. I yelped as she leaped over my head and into the pool. The cold water drenched my breeches as I sat with my eyes scrunched closed.

"Come on in, it feel good!"

Opening my eyes I saw Alex walking down the trail, laughing hysterically, Deiless, in wix form, too, behind him.

Fine. We'll see if he's still laughing when he gets down here. I'm only coming up to my waist, though. Alright, Noctua?

"Me understand."

I told Noctua what I planned and she agreed to do it in less than a heartbeat.

I shook off my cape and jumped in, the water engulfed me up to my stomach.

When Alex walked down far enough, Noctua jumped out of the water and flew up a ways.

I scrambled out of the way as she plummeted to the earth. When she hit the water the largest splash I had ever seen drenched Alex. He froze, his shoulders up, his scrunched up face full of surprise.

I waded and was laughing so hard it was difficult to stay afloat, so I walked to Noctua and sat on her back.

"Oh, you're in for it!" Perl stepped out from behind Alex, soaked too.

I laughed even harder.

Then Alex took off his sword and pack, he and Deiless came splashing in.

Perl took off her cape and joined us, and Timna, too, in wix form.

She was slenderer than Noctua, and a tiny bit shorter, but had just as much energy.

We all splashed each other for a while, careful not to get my arm wet, then just swam around.

"I think I'm gonna go dry off," I told Perl, when I was worn out.

"I'll come with you," she called as I stepped onto a huge, flat, boulder.

I then laid down and spread out my arms to soak up the sun.

I heard Perl lay down next beside me and sigh, "I'm so glad Elyon gave us the sun and warmth, I wouldn't be able to live without it."

I sighed in agreement. After sitting there in the sunlight until my clothes were dry, Teamalie called us to eat. We were up in half a second, finding that we were really hungry from the swim.

"So, Eleny, how long have you had Noctua as a bonded?" Perl asked, then took a bite of her chicken sandwich. We were sitting on our capes on the flat boulder, Teamalie and Grimblon were on a quilt a ways away, and Alex had taken a walk down river with Deiless.

I glanced up at Noctua, she was still in wix form up in a tree talking to Timna. They were making weird growls and whistles.

I looked back at Perl, "It feels like she's been with me my entire life, but actually, only a few moons ago." Then I told her how I met her on the way to Raeya's place.

"Yeah, I've only had Timna as a bonded for about a year, but you're right, it does feel like she's been with me all my life," she smiled softly at Timna, "She's such a good friend."

I nodded, "I don't know if I would be here without Noctua's encouragement. She is so funny sometimes, and she reminds me, like Raeya said, to smell the rosemary along the way," I grinned at the memory.

"Smell the rosemary along the way?" Perl's eyebrows were furrowed, so I told her how I had been learning how to use herbs.

"That's really amazing," she said, when I finished.

"Thanks," I smiled, "It was really fun learning all about herbs." I took a bite of my sandwich, then saw Alex walk up to the Bends and sit next to them. Perl took another bite of her bread.

"It's probably not my place, but why is Alex so secretive?" I asked her.

She focused on him, "I guess it's just his way. Before he started traveling with us, he had to keep his faith hidden from his family because they wouldn't accept Elyon." She sighed, "When they found out about it, they pretty much shunned him. That's why he came and traveled with us in the first place. He was so young, having only been ten years old. I was only eight, so I hadn't realized what happened."

"What? That's not what he said, he said something else. I guess he didn't tell me the whole truth," my mouth sagged to a frown.

She sighed again and looked back at me, "When we came back, three years later, his father's heart had hardened even more. But I also think that they reprimanded that, when they first found out about it, he had mindvoicing abilities. I think he thinks he's, like, not normal, or something."

"Well, he isn't. But that's not for the bad, he should use his gift for good instead of hiding it."

"I know, Eleny, but it isn't really our choice."

I frowned and ate another bite.

When we finished Perl went to her mother and said something to her. She came back to me with Timna on her tail.

I stood and put on my cape, "We're leaving now?"

"Yep."

Before we reached the house, Alex and Grimblon stopped at a cottage.

"What are they doing?" I asked Teamalie.

"I'm afraid I can't tell you." She averted her eyes.

I frowned.

After half an hour of waiting, my curiosity was going crazy, "Why can't you tell me?"

Teamalie gave a hint of a smile, but said nothing.

After a few more minutes passed, they finally jumped back in the wagon. Both of them sat, and I noticed Alex had something wrapped in cloth.

He looked at me and grinned, "Here," he handed it to me, "Open it."

I took and unwrapped it. I gasped at the sight and heat ran up my neck.

It was an Ynit.

"Oh my—" tears came to my eyes, "I was going to pay for it."

Grimblon smiled, "It's alright."

"I don't know what to say."

The hilt was ivory, a barn owl was carved into the elegant wood. The blade itself was a light silver, it shimmered even in the shade of the wagon's sheet.

"How about thank you," Alex grinned.

"I—thank you." I smiled and looked back down at the elegant weapon.

Alex spoke again, "It's hilt is Wixwood, I asked the carpenter to carve Noctua into it. The blade is white silver, the Jinde in Aridon mine it. Happy sixteenth birthing day, Eleny."

My head snapped up, how did he know it was today? Did he look into my mind? I gave him an icy glare.

His hands shot up, "I promise I didn't do what you think I did, it was her," he pointed at Noctua.

Noctua smiled at me. *"Me told Deiless it your birthing day today!"*

"You stinker!" I poked her head.

Every one laughed and said happy birthing day.

I smiled as the wagon started moving, not looking up at Alex's face, for I knew mine was tinted pink.

SIXTEEN

Embarrassment yet Healing

When we reached the house, the other family had already arrived. Perl introduced me to them and they all gave a greeting.

The young mother, which I found her name was Korah Rambey, was sitting with Temmen, the baby boy, in a rocker in the sitting room. The older boy, who I thought was Amalek, was running and yelling through the hallway as the father, Amon Rambey, was tickling the other toddler, Tsuli, as she giggled and screamed.

Perl dragged me straight to her room and then sat on the bed, flustered, and then gave me an apologetic look, "Sorry, sometimes I just can't take the rough housing."

I sat on the chair and nodded, but didn't really know what she meant. *I guess if I were around them all day, I would eventually get tired of their antics. But she's been around them for a few weeks, so I can't imagine how she feels. Either annoyed or just plain worn out.*

She laid down on her bed, then sat up abruptly, "You're probably tired from your trip and then the picnic. I know how it feels to try and sleep on a wagon. It doesn't work." She looked at me, "Do you want to make the pallet now?"

I surprisingly yawned at the thought of laying down. I bit my lip and nodded. She walked out the door and came back with many thick quilts. We stacked the blankets and Perl went to see what everyone else was doing.

I brought out the feather pillow that Raeya gave me as Noctua cuddled up in the covers and I laid down. I decided to talk to Raeya so I closed my eyes.

Eleny Nil to Raeya Pinsa.

"Welcome. Hello Eleny."

I smiled when I heard her voice.

Hi Raeya.

"How have you been, dear?"

The trip was tiring, but today we finally reached Wix Town. Everyone here has a wix.

"I'm glad that you have made it safely."

Not too safely, I'm afraid.

"Why do you say that?"

I told her about the attack and what happened to my arm. We talked until I yawned again and Raeya said I needed to rest. She cut off the connection and I fell asleep.

I heard a rustling, and, rolling over, I saw Perl coming in.

I sat up slowly, "Thanks for letting me sleep for awhile, I didn't get one blink on that wagon."

She nodded knowingly, "I can't sleep on those things either."

"What time is it?"

"Around three."

"How long have I been asleep?"

"About an hour and a half."

I stood as Noctua crawled out from under the quilt. She flew up and landed on my shoulder.

Perl then said, "We're having tea in the sitting room, would you like to join us?"

I grinned, "Sure."

She grabbed a shawl and walked back out the door. I followed and sat down on the sofa next to her. There was a short, but wide, table in the middle of the room. Only Teamalie and Korah were around it.

"Where's A— the others?" I asked as they looked up from their sewing. I was about to say Alex, I'm glad I caught myself.

Teamalie answered, "They're in town getting supplies for when we leave next week."

Then Korah said, "And the little ones're finally takin' a nap, so I get a break," she smiled and glanced up at Noctua, "And I thought that I might as well enjoy the quiet by havin' some tea an' sweets." She then passed me a plate full of cookies. I took one, and sunk my teeth into the soft filling.

"Mm, this is delicious!" I exclaimed.

The young woman beamed, she had light blond hair and a small smile. Her face had a few freckles on her high cheekbones, and she had a strong nose. She wasn't stout, nor skinny, and she was a little bit shorter than me.

When I finished the cookie and some tea, Teamalie stood and walked over to me, "Eleny, do you think it's time to change your bandages?"

I had forgotten about the wound and keeping it clean. "Yes, that's probably a good idea."

"Come to my room, we'll do it in there."

I followed her to a large bedroom that had a big bed, a desk, and sofa.

Teamalie gestured to the plushy piece of furniture, "Go sit there." I sat and she started taking off the strips of cloth. "Oh my goodness."

"What?" I looked and gasped, my arm was almost completely healed, apart from the stitches. "I guess it's time to take out the stitches!" I smiled.

"I guess, but I'm afraid I don't know how to do that."

"I can do it, just give me awhile."

"I best be getting on to dinner," she sighed.

"Maybe I could help later."

"Ooh, me too!" Perl called, walking down the hall, passing the door.

"Oh, girls, that would be very helpful. Thank you," she gave a warm smile and went toward the kitchen, Perl walking behind her.

Noctua hopped off me and landed on the back of a chair. *"Me's going to see what Timna doing."*

Alright, just please be back before dark.

"Oh, no worry. Me not leaving back yard."

Oh, okay.

After using half the hour working on my arm, I stepped into the kitchen and started helping.

When we were done with the dough, we stuck the bread in the oven. Then de-boned some chicken and cooked that too. When we were finished with the peas, the bread was done.

We put out the porcelain plates and potholders on the dining table, the dining room was connected to the kitchen, it had a big window with red drapes.

When we put the food on the table, Amalek, the three year old, and Tsuli, who was five, were already sitting down, ready to eat. Korah then went out and found the men in the small barn, talking, and told them dinner was ready. When they came in everyone else was seated. Everyone commented on the delicious food, which made Teamalie beam.

As we ate I found that Korah had a little

yellow warbler wix, who had bright yellow feathers, and Amon had a red cardinal wix, who had red feathers and a bright orange beak.

When everyone was finished Perl and I cleaned up while they went to the sitting room.

After we were done, we went outside to check on our wixes. They were in wix form, racing above us, and weren't the only ones out. Deiless was playing, too, while Melodia and Mizal were sitting together, watching the young fly back and forth. The sun had already gone down an hour before, the only way you could see was because of the bright moon.

Are you having fun?

"Yes! Yes! Yes!"

She whistled and hooted a few times and then flew down before me. I smiled when she nudged for me to smooth her head feathers.

"Me can sleep in house tonight?"

I frowned and asked Perl as Timna walked up to her, "Um, Noctua can sleep with me in your room tonight, right?"

Her eyebrows went up, "Eleny, you don't think we would let them sleep in the house, do you?"

"Oh, no, no. I, um, I just," I stuttered.

She laughed, "It's fine, I'm pulling your leg. Noctua can be with you, I know how it feels. It's a bond that Elyon created Himself. We can't stop it from happening."

Relieved, I told Noctua and she was pleased that she could sleep in the house. It was getting chillier during the night since the cold season was almost here, so I was glad, too.

A sudden icy wind shot through my clothes and I shivered as Noctua changed back into barn owl form. I lifted up my hood and she flew into it, where she had been when we were coming down the mountain.

"I'm going inside."

Perl glanced back at me, teeth chattering, "Yeah, I'm comin' with you."

We went back to the house to find that the Rambeys had already gone to their inn with their children. The Bends were about to go to bed, too.

Alex was sitting in front of the fireplace, "I'll turn in in a little while," he said when Grimblon asked, staring into the fire.

Soon after Perl's mother and father went to bed, Perl said goodnight to Alex and went to bed, too.

I sat next to him and decided to talk to Alex

about my arm and also why he had lied to me about his family, but before I could figure out how to begin he brought it up.

"So, what's up with your arm?" He pointed at it, "I think I'm the only one that noticed it."

I glanced down at the scab. "Raeya said that you won't find some things in a book, you have to experience them. I think that this is what she was talking about. I can't heal myself, but I do heal faster than others."

He nodded. "That can explain it, but also because you thought quickly and kept it clean, put the right medicines on it."

I shifted my weight from side to side, not knowing what to say to the compliment.

He got to it first, "What's wrong? You look troubled." His face twisted into concern.

"I–um–well–" I couldn't get it out.

"What Eleny?" He turned his whole body to face me.

I took a deep breath and said quietly, "When we went swimming today Perl and I were talking, and she said something that caught me off guard. So I asked her about it, and she told me." I stared at Alex's pale green eyes, "Why did you not tell me the whole truth about your past?"

His face changed from concern to guilt and he turned back to the fireplace, "I-I just don't like it, alright? I've had too many people looking down on me with pity, and I didn't want you to do the same, too." He frowned and looked down between his legs, "Sorry, I should have told you the whole story."

I sighed, "Alex, look at me."

He didn't move.

I grabbed his chin and made his eyes, full of surprise, level with mine.

"First of all, I don't blame you for not telling the whole truth," I sniffed, my eyes filling with tears, "Second of all, I'm really sorry, too, because I didn't tell you the whole truth either, because mine is just as bad. I did tell you I helped a woman out of Patera and that I have a gift. That was true. But it wasn't only me who helped. It was my grandmother and I, that's who I was living with. When I was a baby my mother died, and my father went missing when I was seven," I let go of his face and tears were now streaming down mine as I looked at the fire.

Alex's eyes were now filled with sadness, "What happened to your grandmother?"

I sniffed again as more tears fell, "She took

an arrow for me when we reached the Wall. I've been on my own since then, until, of course, I met Noctua. Then I followed Jone's instructions and found Raeya." I sniffed again and stood, "I'm sorry I just dumped this all on you–" then sobs racked my body.

Alex grabbed my hand, and pulled me into an embrace, "Don't be," he whispered.

"I can't keep it up anymore," I sniffed.

"I know."

"All of this thinking everything will be alright, but my grandmother is gone and things are the way they are."

He stroked my arm, "Things will get better."

"All I wanted to do is tell others about Elyon and be at peace, but these memories keep coming back," I whispered, "I don't have any family now, either."

I cried into his chest and he stroked my back.

His hands were warm, gentle, and strong.

His tunic smelled of fresh rain and mint.

His arms were firm around my back.

After a while of sitting there, I pulled back from him and realized what I just did.

My heart was beating so hard I was sure he

could hear it. My neck and face heated up to where it was like the sun was beating down on me. "Sorry I got you wet, Alex." There was a dark spot on his forest green tunic.

"I'm sorry, I need to go to bed and let you be." I stood and was about to step away, but he grabbed my hand.

"Eleny."

I turned back and looked at him.

"Don't be sorry. If you ever need to pour something out, whether it be words or tears, I know how you feel, I'll be here for you."

I blushed and smiled, "Thank you for listening."

He smiled back, his eyes earnest, "Anytime. Good night, Eleny, sleep well."

"Good night, Alex. The same to you."

I turned quickly, I was tingly all over now, and went to Perl's room, wiping my tears away.

I changed into my nightgown and snuggled under the warm covers with Noctua at my neck, she had been waiting for me in the room. I was so embarrassed of what just happened.

Perl had a bright lantern that lit up the entire room, so it wasn't hard to see.

She was sitting up in her bed, having her

nightgown on too, and brushing her reddish auburn hair. When she was finished she stood and set it on her dresser then got back in bed.

"Why are you traveling with us?" she asked, leaning up on her elbow.

"What do you mean?"

Her eyebrows furrowed, "I mean, like, how did you get to this Raeya woman? Is she a relative? Some old friend?"

When I didn't answer right away she said quickly, "I'm sorry, it wasn't my place. I tend to speak before I think, it runs in the family."

"No, it's fine." I took a breath, it was still ragged from earlier, "Raeya was a friend of a friend's when I first met her. Why I went to her? Well, there are many reasons."

Perl turned out the light, then laid down and listened as I told her about how I helped Palana out of Patera, then how I found Jone and Raeya.

Then the realization hit me. These gifts were Elyon's that he gave. Patera didn't want Elyon's men teaching. Elyon's Word, I bet, was forbidden. The reason I had never heard of Him was because Grandmother had probably been forbidden to tell anyone about Him, but she still believed. That's why she probably, if she knew about it, never told me about my gift. Because it would have endangered me if I knew. Why was it law to kill people with the gifts? Why had these things been forbidden? Why would they do this? *Who* would do this? Who was behind all of this?

Then the darkness, the feeling I had when I thought of the raids the day I healed Jone, came back over me when I thought about it. I had bet that they were the ones behind the raids. But why take babies? Infants? Why? It all felt connected somehow.

"Eleny, are you alright?"

I saw that Perl was sitting up in her bed, staring at me.

I shook out of my train of thought, "Uh, yeah, yeah."

"Are you sure?"

"Yes, I'm alright, where was I?"

"You were at the part of the cottage you found."

"Oh, well we stayed there until I left with your parents," I said, and then continued on in the story and what happened.

Then I told Perl about my mindvoicing abilities, knowing that I could trust her.

Wow Eleny, trust her? You didn't tell her about your grandmother.

She sighed, "I wish I had those abilities."

"Didn't you know that I can connect to you and we can talk?"

"You can?" she sat up.

"Yes, you can't connect to me, but you can talk to me if *I* connect to you."

"Oh, can we do it now?"

"Sure, when you hear my name pop up in your head, say 'welcome'."

"Got it."

Eleny Nil to Perlelia Bend.

I heard her gasp. *"Welcome! I'm talking without moving my mouth!"*

I chortled. *yep.*

"Whoa!"

She paused for a second. *"I wonder why Alex never did this with me before."*

I'm afraid I don't know. Hmm, maybe he didn't know that you could.

She shrugged.

"Hey Perl, so you've known Alex since you were eight?" I asked.

"Yeah," she answered, "We pretty much grew up together. I actually had a crush on him when I was ten," She chuckled, "But don't worry, I'm definitely over it. We're more like brother and sister than anything else."

That answered my thoughts.

I yawned, "I'm going to sleep."

"Yeah, me too. We need to rest, because I'm taking you somewhere great tomorrow."

"Where?"

"You'll see."

SEVENTEEN

The Colony

    Soaring through the sky with Noctua underneath me was one of the best feelings in the world.

    Perl hadn't told me where we were going, only that I would love it.

    Timna was in front of me now, zooming and making sharp turns, back and forth. It was hard for Noctua and Deiless to keep up with the flexible wix.

    Alex and Deiless were above us, flying in and out of the clouds.

I couldn't stop thinking about what happened last night. I shivered at the memory of Alex's arms around me. I was glad Noctua didn't mention any of it when we talked, it felt too awkward.

Noctua turned her head to look at me. *"It hard to keep up with both of them."*

I nodded and scratched her long, soft, fur. *You're just out of practice, we've been traveling in a wagon for a few days and you haven't been in wix form at all.*

"No, me just don't go this high often."

We'll be flying a lot more when we travel, don't worry.

"Yes! Me like being up here." She flapped a few times to gain speed.

I had slept well the night before and this morning we had some sweet bread and eggs that Teamalie made for breakfast. It got a little awkward with Alex so we didn't talk much. I had asked Perl multiple times where we're going, but she wouldn't even answer. I had even been tempted to peek into her mind, but I resisted, knowing that it would ruin the surprise and that I could lose her trust.

We were now flying over the plains

surrounding Wix Town. It looked as if the people had already harvested for the season, the fields were bare as the sun shone down on them. Even though the sun was out, the blue sky was beautiful and there were few clouds, it was cooler than the day before.

    Shivering, I pulled my cape closer and lifted my hood.

    I then connected to Perl. *Eleny Nil to Perlelia Bend.*

    "Welcome. Goodness, Eleny! You scared me half to death!"

    I laughed out loud. *Sorry for frightening you, but it's not like I can talk to you out loud up here with the wind.*

    "Yeah, it's pretty windy up here."
    Um, I was going to ask you, are we almost there?
    "Just a little bit farther."

    I cut the connection and peered around Noctua, we were still a ways behind Timna. I looked down, now we were over some low hills covered in tall, golden, grass.

    I glanced back at Perl and Timna, they were descending, and Alex and Deiless, who were beside us, were too. I looked down again, still over the hills. Where were we going?

That was when I noticed that the ground was... shimmering? I rubbed my eyes, then looked at Alex.

He was gone. Perl was gone too.

"Perl! Alex!" I shouted, starting to panic.

"Alexovin Hendruton to Eleny Nil."

Welcome. Where did you go?

"Just fly straight down."

What do you mean? There's nothing here but fields!

"Just do it, you'll see in a minute if you fly straight down. Trust me."

Trust him? That felt like a little bit more than it sounded. But I did trust him. I trusted him. *Okay...*

The connection cut.

Alright Noctua, did you hear him?

"Yes, me did."

Then let's go.

She started to descend. I squeezed on tight as we dove closer to the ground.

Then something happened. Everything slowed down. I opened my eyes to see sparkles around us.

When we descended faster again, I closed my eyes.

"Open your eyes!"

Fine.

Opening my eyes, I saw that there was a huge rainbow all around me.

No, wait. Rainbows don't move.

Then my eyes cleared and I gasped. It wasn't a rainbow.

Wixes. Hundreds of wixes of all colors were on the ground and flying in the air.

Do you see Timna or Deiless?

"No, we need to land."

I nodded.

When Noctua touched the ground, I slid off, not noticing how tall the grass was. When I hit the dirt, the grass was up to my shoulders!   Wixes were throughout the hills.

I looked back at Noctua. *I think I might need to stay on you.*

"Me think so too."

I jumped back on and stood up on her, using her head for support.

"What was that? The sparkles we went through?"

Maybe a barrier?

"But you couldn't see it from the air! That was so weird!"

I then searched the horizon and spotted

Timna. She was coming our way with Perl on her back.

I laughed when she had to dodge a few wixes on the way but then got smacked in the face with a tail.

Perl finally reached me, "Come on, Eleny! We want to show you something amazing!"

She turned back around and Timna took off into the air. I sat back down on Noctua and we were right behind her.

We flew a few minutes before she stopped and landed in a clearing. Surrounding the patch of dirt were large craters in the tall grass. We landed and I saw that Alex was approaching one.

"Alex, wait for us!" Perl whispered-shouted.

We jumped up off of Timna and Noctua and ran to him.

"What are we doing?" I asked.

Alex had a mischievous grin on his face and jumped into the shallow crater, "Come on."

Perl hopped down, too, so I followed again. They both crouched down over a clump of grass and moved it. Underneath were two speckled eggs.

I gasped, "Are those…"

Perl smiled, "Yes. Wix eggs. They hatch

next spring. The mother and father take turns sitting on the eggs in wix form for eight moons out of the year. Then they feed and care for the young for about five moons until they can turn into their bird form." she touched the blue egg, then the brown, "You normally can't tell exactly what bird they are until they can turn into bird form. I mean, you can guess by the colors and patterns, but it's never accurate. There are so many kinds of birds."

Alex's hand landed on my back and it seized up.

Trying to ignore it, I nodded then froze, "What about these eggs' mother and father?" I jerked my head up.

Alex replied, making eye contact with me for the first time today, "We know the parents, and we asked them first."

Relieved, I asked, "What would have happened if we came here without asking?"

They shared nervous glances.

"Lets just say that it would be bad," Alex muttered, then dropped the subject, "Would you like to see some of the young that hatched last spring?"

"Yes. A definite yes," I grinned.

They led me to another nest and we

jumped in again.

At first there wasn't any movement. Then something caught my eye. I swerved and there was a wix nudging my leg, but the smallest I'd ever seen, not that I'd seen many. It was up to my knee, the size of a small dog.

I knelt down and touched its blue head, it sneezed and I laughed. The little wixen's horns were gray, but the rest of him or her, was a vibrant sky blue. I glanced up to see Perl and Alex staring at me.

"What?"

"The wixen never let people touch them," Perl squeaked.

"Never, they always run away," Alex started toward me and the little wixen.

I stood up and it ran behind me.

Alex stopped walking and looked up at me, "That's peculiar," then he went around to the other side of me.

As he did the creature went around the other way.

"Huh," Alex backed up to the other end of the nest, Perl watching.

The wixen came back from behind me, then sat at my feet, nose up, as I asked, "Can it fly yet?"

"No," Alex said, then chuckled, eyebrows raised, "That's different," he turned to Perl, "Why don't *you* try? I want to see something."

She nodded at him, then stepped slowly to me. I could see that the wixen was eyeing her nervously, then it squeezed between my legs and sat behind me again. I stifled a laugh when Perl frowned.

"Ha! I have no idea why he's doing that, like I said, they've always run away," Alex threw his hands up in the air.

"So it's a boy?" I knelt down again and stroked his head, "I wonder what his name is."

Hey, Noctua?

"Yes? Me is with Timna and Deiless, me meet their friends."

Oh, that's great! Can you come here?

"Yes, wait a moment."

A minute later, she dropped into the nest gently. The wixen ran up to her and started tweeting and growling.

"It so cute!"

What is his name?

"He doesn't have a name yet because he still only a wixen. When wixen are old enough they turn into wix, *right? Well, that's when they get their name."*

Well then for now let's just call him Little Blue.

"Good idea."

She bent her head down and whistled a few times. The wixen replied by jumping up on Noctua, paws on her head, and tweeted.

I smiled and sat down next to him, cross legged. He crawled down low, then jumped in my lap and curled up. Perl gasped and I gestured for her to come closer.

"Alex," I whispered, "Come here."

As he came closer, too, I grabbed his hand and pulled him down next to me, blushing, by how I did it.

His face tinted pink, then he smiled as he sat by my side and touched the little blue head as the wixen was asleep.

"He's so soft!" Perl whispered.

I smiled, "I really don't know why he likes me so."

Perl shrugged and kept stroking the wixen's blue wings, "The mother and father sometimes leave their wixen for a while to hunt."

I nodded, then watched Alex stand, jump out, and jog to Deiless.

I jumped when I heard a loud thump behind

me, and turning my head I saw two wixes. One was black, the other was green, blue, and yellow. They started to growl low at us, claws showing, and took some steps forward, but then the little blue wixen ran off my lap and started yipping and tweeting happily to them.

Eleny Nil to Perlelia Bend.

Perl answered. *"Welcome."*

You did *ask if we could come in here. Right?*

"Uh... no?"

The creatures bent down and each twittered back at him. After they stopped and lifted their heads, they walked up to us and sniffed our hair, then necks. When they were satisfied and laid down, Noctua joined them, all of them tweeting and twittering.

Phew, that was close to being really bad.

"You can say that again."

Little blue tromped back to us and played with us for a while, but then we saw that the sun was high. It was probably around two o'clock, and I was starving. Well, maybe not starving, just so hungry that my stomach was telling me it was time to eat.

"I think it's time to go back," Perl said, as if reading my mind. She stood and walked to the edge of the nest, then turned back to me, "I'll call Timna, you get Noctua."

"Okay."

Hey, Noctua.

She turned her head my way. *"We leaving now?"*

Yes.

"Oh. Alright."

She stood sheepishly and walked to my side. I turned back to see Little Blue step curiously to me, head cocked.

"What sweet thing."

He made some tweets, then bolted to his parents, trying to flap along the way. When he reached them, he turned back around, as if to say good bye.

"Bye Little Blue." I waved.

I hopped onto Noctua and we were off again, heading back.

We were flying lower to the ground this time, over the bare fields again. The day had heated up quite a lot since we first started out that morning.

After gliding slowly for a while, I started hearing some fast flapping. I looked at Timna and Deiless, who were only flapping a couple times every few minutes, and decided it was my imagination.   Noctua turned her head to look at me. *"Me no feel right."*

What's wrong?

"Me no know, but it something bad."

Wait, I thought it was my imagination, but do you hear something?

"Hmm, me think me hear wing beats. But not Timna's or Deiless's wing beats."

I searched our surroundings, and saw a little speck in the distance behind us. *Elyon imi kudoz.*

Noctua, stop!

She quit flapping and turned abruptly.

Do you see it?

"Yes."

She took off at break-neck speed toward it. When it came into view, I gasped.

It was a wixen.

It was Little Blue.

EIGHTEEN

Destruction yet New Growth

Noctua ...
"Me knew something wrong."
What's wrong?
"We see. He said to follow him."
So we followed him. I glanced back and saw Alex and Perl following, too.
"Alexovin Hendruton to Eleny Nil."
Welcome.
"What are you doing?"
I'm not sure yet.

"Why are you going back?"

Still not sure yet, but it's something bad.

"What does that mean?"

Okay, if you keep asking questions like this, I'm not answering them. We need to go back for a reason that I don't know yet.

"Well, we're right behind you."

Good, we might need it.

When I came out the other side of the barrier I was horrified.

All of the rainbow was gone. Or at least, some of it laid in pieces. When Noctua landed on the small clearing, I fell on the dirt and broke into a sob.

Almost all of the wixes were gone or dead. Instead of wasting time shedding tears, I stood to look in the nests. The eggs were gone, too. So were all of the wixen. Little Blue came up to me and nudged for me to follow. He led me to his nest. Inside were his parents.

I closed my eyes and turned away at the sight. I walked numbly back to the clearing and sat down on the dirt. The little wixen curled up in my lap as I cried. What had happened?

I then heard a swoosh behind me. Without looking up, I knew that it was Perl.

She sniffed a few times and sat beside me, "None alive. Alex and I searched for survivors, but found none," she wiped her nose with her sleeve and let out a whimper. "Oh Eleny, why would something like this happen?" she said, then jumped up on Timna and they flew off.

I couldn't move. Even when Alex said something to me, I couldn't hear him. I finally jumped when Noctua nudged me.

"Me need to ask Little Blue what happen."

I nodded and patted him softly on the back. He moved a little bit, then sat up. That was when I saw that his wing was twisted and feathers bent. Noctua whistled and growled a few times and Little Blue answered. This went on for a few minutes.

Noctua then sat down and looked at me solemnly.

"He say that he see black things in the distance, in the sky. He no see what happened. He say his mother and father told him to fly away, he didn't look back, but heard the growling and howling and claws coming out. The flying was very hard, for he hadn't done it before. Then he hear shouts, people shouts. When we saw him, his wings hurt very much. It took a lot of courage to come back. Before he was able to land, his wings stopped working, and he fell a short ways and crashed."

That still doesn't explain what happened.

"All he know is that no wixen or egg was killed, only taken."

I wonder why.

I then looked back at Little Blue's wings, they looked bad, but not severe enough to use my gift. I instead pulled out my box and took out my herbs and bandages. I laid a blanket on the ground and gave the wixen something to make him sleep. When he ate it, a few minutes later he was snoring softly.

I worked quickly, first cleaning the wound and his wings. Then I put the twisted wing back into place, wrapping it in the strip of cloth. When I finished that, I put a salve on his wound, and wrapped it tightly, too.

After I sat back, someone whistled behind me. Turning my head around, I saw that it was Alex.

He stepped closer, "Are you sure you've only been training for a moon?"

"Mm hmm."

He whistled again as I looked back at my work. I guess it did look pretty good, considering it was my first time treating a wound this bad.

I looked back at Alex, "I have to bring him."

He didn't say anything for a moment, then finally nodded, "We need to get back, I'll go get Perl." He turned and got on his wix.

The little wixen in my lap was whimpering, so I stroked his neck. He stopped, but still moaned every few minutes.

Not wasting time, I wrapped him up in the blanket like you would a babe. Alex soon came back with Perl by his side, she had puffy eyes and red cheeks.

She gave a frown and jumped off of Timna, "You need me to help you get up on Noctua?"

"Sure," I stood and gave her Little Blue to jump up on my wix. When I was secure, Perl passed the wixen back to me.

Even though Little Blue was asleep, not making a single noise, the flight was long. I couldn't stop thinking that everyone wouldn't let me keep the little one while I traveled with the Bends and Rambeys.

We walked across the the porch, Noctua sitting on my shoulder, never taking her eyes off of Little Blue, and went to the door. Grimblon was reading a book and Teamalie was sewing when we stepped in. When Teamalie saw that I was carrying something, she jumped up and came to see what.

She gasped, "What-"

Then Perl looked at me.

Eleny Nil to Perlelia Bend.

"Welcome, you can go to my room."

Thanks.

I started down the hall as Perl went off, and put Little Blue on my pallet. Then came back to the living space, Perl was telling them everything, from how Little Blue played with me, to what we saw. Then Perl asked if I could care for Little Blue.

Grimblon frowned, "I guess, as long as it isn't any trouble."

"No, he won't be any trouble to you at all, I promise." I said with determination.

He nodded, "Then you can care for him, Eleny."

"Thank you," I turned and went to the room, Perl following.

I unwrapped the blue wixen. He sat up and peered at me, then around the room. Then he turned and curled back up in the blanket. Noctua cuddled next to him.

I frowned and decided to leave him there, then sat on Perl's bed next to her. Sighing, I brought out my box and whispered, "Library," the tall, long cabinet folded out. I opened it and saw that Raeya had packed all six shelves with books. I smiled and spotted a book labeled "Wixogy". I grabbed the wix book and flipped through the pages. I stopped when I saw what I needed and read aloud.

"'How to care for wixen' by Zerah Johm.

"Wixen can't take care of themselves so you have to be with them almost all day. You can only leave them if they are in an environment where they can't get hurt, and where they can't get into things. Always know where the wixen is. They get into trouble very quickly and easily. They all have different time habits, they could be hyper in the morning or the evening, and they all eat three times a day. When awake, they are excited and curious, but they sleep a lot and need their rest, just like a babe.

"If it doesn't eat what you give it, and you don't have a wix to find out what's wrong, try different things. If it likes what you give it, remember what ingredients were in it, it might like similar foods. The normal foods that the mother and father bring it are raw meats from the hunt, and vegetables from the forest. When a wixen can turn into bird form, now an adult calling it a wix, it's food type changes to what that bird eats. For example, if it turns to a sparrow, then it's food would change to seeds and insects, instead of meat and vegetables.

"If you have a wix, the wixen needs to spend time with it and teach it how to speak English. If you do not have a wix, you may become it's bonded, even if you didn't want to. The most important of all, is that it…" I paused and looked up at Perl, "that it will likely become your bonded if you raise it."

Her eyes widened, "You can have a second bonded?"

I shrugged and flipped a few more pages, "I think a few people in this book have had a second, either that or they lived with the wixes in their colony."

"Hmm."

I glanced up, realizing Alex was in the room looking at me. I shrugged again to relax myself, shaking the warmth off, "Either way, I'm going to take care of him until he is old enough to be on his own. No matter what."

Alex stared more intently, "It's going to be hard, Little Blue can't turn into bird form yet."

"According to how old he is now, we should be able to determine when he'll be able to."

"I have to admit, I hadn't thought of that," Alex peered down at the wixen, then walked over to me and held my shoulder, "Are you sure you're up to it?" His eyes were piercing, he was probably remembering last night, like I was.

I swallowed, "Yes."

His face became more concerned and he lifted an eyebrow.

"Yes, I said yes, Alex!" I rolled my eyes.

He sighed and retrieved his hand, "Alright."

I watched as Little Blue stretched and nervously glanced around. When he saw me he perked up a little and walked up to me to jump in my lap.

I then stifled a full on laugh as both Alex and Perl watched, jaw dropped and eyes as big as saucers.

I glanced back down, Little Blue was leaning against my chest, more peaceful now that he was sitting with me. His bright blue head was glowing in the sunlight.

Noticing how far the sun was down, my stomach started growling, "I hadn't noticed how much time had passed, I haven't eaten all day."

"Me neither," Perl said, heading for the door, "I'm going to help Mother with dinner."

"I'm coming."

She turned around, "But you have to stay with Little Blue."

Right. I guess I could bring him with me, he could be on my shoulder.

I shook my head, "It's fine, I've got him."

"How about you just set the table, then?"

Perl probably wouldn't let me win, so I gave in and nodded.

She turned back and walked down the hall.

"Are you really okay, Eleny?" Alex moved to the door.

"Alex, remember how you said you don't want people pitying you?"

He nodded.

"Well, you're doing that right now to me. The reason I told you those things last night weren't so that you would pity me. It was about me showing you apart of my life that I don't show everybody and trusting one another. I'm not some fragile child to watch over."

Alex frowned and the worry line appeared between his eyebrows again, "Eleny, I don't see you as a child. In fact, I see you as one of the bravest and strongest people I know. Helping someone out of a bad place? Keep going even though you have nothing to keep going for? Traveling all by yourself? Using your gift even if it meant risking your safety?" He looked at my eyes, "and I don't pity you, that's not why I asked if you're alright. I asked," He knelt down in front of me so our faces were level, "because I'm beginning to care about you."

I froze, "But Alex, we're of different races, you're a Xelman, I'm a Thasfaen." I pointed at myself and him.

He shook his head, disgusted, "Do you think I care about *that*?" His face was questioning, "But I want to know if you're feeling this way about me, too. If you don't, I'll shut up."

I gazed into his pale green eyes that were flecked with silver, "I– I don't know. We've just recently met. I need to think, Alex. . .Okay?"

He frowned and nodded, "Okay."

Before I could say anything else he stood and started walking towards the door, "Grimblon says he can start teaching you the Ynit tomorrow," then he turned back to me, "I think it's really great that you're taking care of the little wixen, Eleny."

I nodded, touching the hilt of the small sword as he walked down the hall.

After he left, it was just me, Noctua, and

Little Blue.

I sighed, almost numb from shock. Then I shook the feeling away to deal with my emotions later. I had a wixen to take care of. *Noctua?*

She stood up abruptly and flapped her wings with half closed eyes. *"What what? Who took my mouse?"*

I waved to get her attention. *Noctua.*

She stopped flapping and noticed me.

I need you to tell Little Blue to get on my shoulder when I snap my fingers, that's the way I could say to get up.

"Okay."

She flew to my shoulder then looked to Little Blue. They must have been mindvoicing, because they made no movement or sound. Little Blue turned his head to me. I snapped my fingers and he jumped up on the other shoulder.

"Yes!" I said, not realizing I had voiced my thought. Excited over the accomplishment, I walked out the door toward the dining room.

After I set the table, I remembered that the wixen couldn't feed himself, unlike how Noctua went hunting.

Noctua, like always, read my mind. *"Me going to hunt while you feed Little Blue. Me say to him that you going to feed him something and me be back later."*

Thank you, I'll see you after dinner.

She flew off my shoulder and through the window. Little Blue gave a little whimper, so I stroked his silky head and it soothed him just as it did with Noctua.

I walked into the kitchen, "Hey."

"Hey." Perl said.

"Do you have any left over meat?"

She nodded, but then frowned, "It's cooked, is that okay?"

I bit my lip and my eyebrows furrowed, "I think so."

"Alright..." she went and grabbed a bowl that had some beef in it. She took some and gave it to me.

I lifted it up on the palm of my hand and we waited a second. Little Blue peered at it suspiciously, then took a little piece. After swallowing he scarfed down the rest.

Perl exclaimed when he finished the whole bowl, "He must have liked it!"

"I'm so glad! I was worried that he wouldn't," I smoothed his feathers and he leaned into my hand.

The rest of the night Little Blue and Noctua were on my shoulders, interested in whatever I was doing, from cleaning, to playing with the toddlers, to even just talking with the others.

During dinner Alex was across from me. I averted my eyes from him, because I didn't know what else to do.

When I went to bed, Noctua, as usual, was at my neck, and Little Blue was curled up at my torso. The little wixen whistled softly when I smoothed his head feathers. Then I smoothed Noctua's.

You know, Noctua, I hadn't asked you what you thought about caring for this little wix.

"Me like Little Blue very much, me and him talked a lot. Me would love to take care of him, too."

What did you talk about?

"About how me lose my mother. Me want Little Blue to grow with a mother."

I know how it feels. I don't want him to grow without a mother either.

"Maybe me and you can mother him together! Me want to be a mother to him, but me can't do it by myself."

Well, I can't do it by myself either. So I'm going to need you to help by teaching him my language, communicating for me, and keeping him out of trouble.

"He talks your language well. He very smart and learn fast. His age too young to fly, but he did. He too young to know your language, but speak it well. His mother and father teach him early, me would have, too."

Alright, that's great. Good night, Noctua.

"Good night."

NINETEEN

Training for both Girl and Wixen

"Aha!" I exclaimed, "I think I've got it!"

Grimblon nodded, showing a smile, "Yes, you're getting the hang of it. But you need to tighten yourself in more when you roll."

Grimblon had been teaching me how to roll from a standing position since the dawn. I looked up, it was around noon, perhaps past.

Noctua and Little Blue were watching, perched up in a maple tree. The red leaves made Noctua's feathers seem orange. Corvus was on the branch above them.

As I stood Grimblon spoke again, "Next I'll teach you how to end up standing, instead of sitting on the ground, this is good for when you need to get behind your opponent. Like when he has a shield."

He put one foot behind him, then, giving him momentum, took a few steps and jumped, hit the ground, rolled a few feet, then jumped back up to a stand, turning around lightning fast.

I watched in awe, "Whoa."

He stepped back to the house and stroked his blond beard, "Now, after that, I'm to teach you how to roll in the air, hit the ground with your feet, stand, and spin around. This is good for when you are surrounded, you can jump over the opponents."

I nodded, "Got it."

"After that, I'll teach you some more moves. But for now, you just need to learn to roll from a standing position. Try again."

I took a step back, ran a few steps, dove, then tucked my legs and head in. I ended up sitting. "So how do I end up on my feet?"

"When you're rolling, you need to push down your feet before you finish rolling."

I nodded again, then tried what he instructed. I rolled, pushed down my feet, and sort of jumped up. Sweat was dripping down my face, I swiped it off with my sleeve and gasped, "How was that?"

Alex was standing next to Grimblon, who was grinning, "Well done! You are a quick learner."

"Yes, but now," Alex smirked, as if nothing happened yesterday. "it's time to learn how to use those maneuvers in fighting with the Ynit." He strode over to me and unsheathed a wooden sword, "You want to be light on your feet. I'm going to swipe left to hit your ankle, you need to jump up over it."

I nodded, "Ready."

He swiped down, but as I hopped up, he hit my foot and I fell on my bum.

Alex gasped and bent down, his face turned red, "I'm so sorry—"

"It's alright, it's alright!" I grabbed his hand as I stood back up, "I didn't push off soon enough. Again."

He was hesitant, but hit left again.

This time I jumped high enough and missed his swipe. I grinned.

So did Alex, "Now right."

When he hit right, I jumped up and he missed.

"Good work," said Grimblon.

Teamalie was behind him, smiling, too, "Wonderful. It's past lunch, you both have to be starving. I saved some chicken for you, come on inside."

I snapped my fingers for Little Blue and followed them to the house.

After I ate the food, I found Perl in her room, looking out the window.

"Hey, what're you up to?" I asked.

She looked up at me, "Nothing, just thinking. So you're learning the Ynit?"

I nodded.

"My father taught me dagger, but I never really use it." She stepped over to her dresser and picked up and blade from a drawer. She held it up, it had a swirly design on the holster. "I also learned how to throw it, I've only used it on targets, though."

"Well, this is for emergencies, really. Not for sports. But the flipping and rolling is fun."

"Yeah, I bet." I sat beside her. Little Blue hopped down and curled up on my blanket.

"Hey, you want get a snack?" Perl stood. "I

could go for an apple right about now."

"Sure, I'll come, too."

We walked to the kitchen and found a basket full of apples and oranges.

I grabbed an orange and started peeling, then took a slice of the fruit.

Mm, *haven't had one of these in a while.*

"Ooo, can me try a bite?" Noctua, on my shoulder, clacked her beak.

Sure. I peeled of a piece and gave it to her.

She took it and, head lifted back, gulped. Then a tremor went up her spine. *"Ugh, me do NOT like that. Why is it COLD? Me like warm things to eat, like mice. Why you LIKE that?"*

I laughed. *Um, maybe because of the flavor?*

"Ew, me no like the flavor either."

Let's go see if Little Blue wants to try it.

I turned to Perl, who was already almost done with her apple, "I'm heading back to your room."

"Okay, I'm going to see what mother is doing. See you later."

I nodded and went back through the hall.

When I opened the door I gasped. The blankets that had made up my pallet were strewn everywhere, on Perl's bed, on her dresser, across the floor, just everywhere!

"*Oh no...*" Noctua's eyes were big and her beak was open.

Oh no is right.

I searched the room and saw Little Blue's shape under one of the blankets.

I frowned and bent over him, "Little Blue?"

His head poked out and he slowly crawled from underneath the quilt. And I was glad I wasn't in his shoes from what happened next.

Noctua jumped down and started screeching like crazy at him, flapping her wings, walking back and forth. I'd never seen her act this way before.

I decided not to interrupt her, myself not wanting to be in the line of fire.

His wings drooped and he looked down.

When her monologue ended I asked her. *What all did you say?*

"*Me say that he a very bad little wixen, that you cared for him and he turn and be mean.*"

It sounded like more than that.

"*Me also say he would be lucky if you keep him after this, and if he does anything like this again me is going to call him a goggletog from now on.*"

What. In. The. World. Is. A. Goggletog?

"It's a big, mean, green monster that bullies others. But don't worry, they not real, they're just wix tales."

Ha, so that's what they use to scare little wixen from getting into trouble?

"Yep."

We'd better start cleaning up before Perl comes in here, tell Little Blue that he's going to help.

"Okay."

I knelt and picked up a blanket, then spread it out where my pallet used to be. Noctua flew up to the dresser to grab the quilt draped over the mirror. I turned to see Little Blue sheepishly dragging a blanket off the bed to where I was sitting, near the pallet.

When we were done stacking the blankets Little Blue came up to me, hanging his head and gave a sad whistle, as if to apologize.

I patted his head, "It's alright, you're still staying with me. I forgive you."

He looked up at me and grinned, tweeting, then jumped up and put his paws around my neck.

I stroked his velvety soft back, blaming myself for the mess. I had just read in a book not to leave a wixen alone, even for a minute.

Which is exactly what I did.

After the room was cleaned all the way, we went outside to join Perl and Timna for a flight.

TWENTY

Traveling to Riverport

The rest of the week everybody had the same routine.

Except for me. I had a wixen to care for and even though Noctua was helping me, it still took a lot of work, like Alex said.

After cleaning Little Blue's wound, while he wriggled the entire time, it healed up completely by the end of the week. Now we played outside, played inside, and, now, played up in the air. Noctua taught Little Blue and I took care of him. Little Blue ate when I ate, and slept when I slept.

Grimblon and Alex were teaching me to fight with the Ynit almost every day. I now knew how to flip sideways, forwards, and even backwards, in the air and land on my feet. I started learning how to jab Alex from the side, behind, and below—with a stick, of course.

But I was still trying to figure out how I *felt* about Alex. Unless we were in combat, it got awkward and we didn't know what to say to each other anymore.

When we were packing up to leave the two wixes were on my shoulders, watching my every move. I made sure to bring the meat leftover from the night before for Little Blue.

We were all traveling on our wixes. Little Blue was going to fly with Noctua sometimes, but most of the trip he was going to be in my lap.

We were going to River Port, which would take a few days to get there on foot or wagon, but since we had wixes? We were going to get there tomorrow, and I smiled as I thought about it. Especially because I didn't have to ride in a bumpy wagon.

Don't get me wrong, I was thankful Zepho gave us a ride. I just liked traveling by wix more, it was faster and less bumpy. Relaxing. I couldn't wait to be above the clouds again. We hadn't been as high as the clouds since the wix colony.

"Hey, are you ready to go?"

I turned to see Perl poking her head in.

"Yep, I'm coming," I snapped my fingers and Little Blue jumped up on my shoulder. Noctua, too. She learned that when I snapped my fingers for Little Blue to get up, it normally meant I was leaving the room and she wanted a ride, too. Which I didn't mind, she barely weighed anything so sometimes I forgot she was even there. I also enjoyed her enthusiastic company.

I closed up my box and followed Perl down the hallway. Her mother had told her about the folding box a few days before, and amazed was she. Teamalie even made a box for Perl like I did for her and Grimblon! I then decided to make one for Amon and Korah, too, to make it easier. They did have three little ones, so their luggage had to be difficult to travel with.

When Perl and I reached the back door and stepped outside, I saw that everyone had packed their things and were ready to go. The sun was high and few clouds were out. There was a breeze and Noctua said, which I relayed to Grimblon, that there was an air current right outside of town that we could fly in.

Noctua hopped off and turned into her

golden wix form. I jumped up on her then Little Blue plopped down in my lap, so I scratched his neck feathers.

"Alright, everyone ready?"

I glanced over at Corvus to see that Grimblon was speaking.   Everybody was on their wixes nodding, ready to go.

Grimblon on Corvus, Teamalie on Melodia, and Perl on Timna. Amon, who had Temmen, was on his red cardinal wix, Nalis. Korah had her little girl strapped around her waist, shifting on her yellow warbler wix, Petechia. Alex had their toddler Amalek, and was bouncing his legs up and down to make the little one laugh.

Grimblon took off, then Alex, Teamalie, Amon, Perl, Korah, then me. Grimblon told me that we, Noctua and I, were to be at point to lead the way to the air current.

When we got to it he and Corvus flew point and led until lunch where we stopped near Way River. While we ate, the wixes rested and hunted. After we were all done, we left again, flying nonstop until sunset.

"Me tell you one thing, me sleep good tonight. I not even have energy to hunt."

I laughed when Noctua fell backward in my lap, talons up in the air, exhausted. Little Blue was curled up beside me in the blankets, whistling when exhaling.

We had landed about an hour ago and set up camp. Now we were all around the fire, except for the little ones, who were fast asleep in their tent.

I shivered and pulled the blanket tighter around my arms, "It sure is chilly tonight."

Perl, who was a few feet away, agreed, "The cold season is almost here."

"I miss the warmth already," added Alex, who was a few feet away on the opposite side of me, his black hair messy, his forest green tunic wrinkled.

Nodding, I yawned, and laid down.

I woke up, it was dawn. Noctua was curled up at my waist with Little Blue.

But something was warm on the opposite side from where they were. I turned to see and my heart lurched.

Alex's arm was stretched out across the few feet that separated our mats and his hand was resting on my mat, against my side.

I wanted to jump out of bed, but decided to sit up slowly and scoot off of the fabric.

I smiled. *Clumsy Xelman.*

It would probably embarrass him if he saw what he did, so I stood and took a walk in the woods.

I sighed with relief that everyone was up and around when I got back.

"We should be there by mid-afternoon," Grimblon announced.

Everybody was packed up and the wixes were turning into their other form. I was in awe as I gawked at Petechia, whose light was a sunny yellow, and Nalis, whose was a bright red. I hadn't seen them transform yet. Neither Corvus and Melodia's. Melodia's light was a soft white with some brown streaked in, Corvus' was silver and black.

We crossed the river after a while, then all you could see were bare fields. In the distance you could see the peak of Raeya's valley. I missed her so.

When the sun was high we had a quick lunch, eager to reach River Port.

Little Blue was flying beside us when I saw a line of blue-green on the horizon.

Noctua shuddered with excitement. *"It's the sea!"*

We'll be at River Port soon.

"Me can't wait to land, me getting tired."

I bet.

I glanced around to see Amon and Korah pointing at the waves for their little ones to know where to look.

Perl's eyes were solemn, I had noticed that she hadn't even smiled since the wix colony. I had tried to talk to her about it a few times, but she would drop the subject.

Grimblon started descending, when we came closer to the town, in a little field.

We all hopped down after Grimblon, and the wixes turned to bird form. Little Amalek and Tsuli started chasing each other, glad to be free.

"Stay near," Amon said sternly to the children, "we don't want yeh to get lost."

Little Blue plopped down in the grass and rolled in it.

As we walked into town the little wixen strolled beside me as Noctua took a nap in my hood.

I hurried up and walked next to Alex, and couldn't help the thinking of my side that was burning from where he touched, "What are we going to do now that we're here?"

He glanced down at me, "We will help anyone who needs help. You girls and Korah and Teamalie will probably talk with the other women, about Elyon and such. Us men will do the same, but with the men."

Ha, I was not a just a girl. I wasn't a full grown women yet, but I was not a little girl, a little girl would be Tsuli. Maybe if I was taller like a Xelman he would accept me a little better.

But then I remembered how he said I was one of the bravest people he knew. My stomach started having butterflies at the thought.

He acted as though Perl was a little girl, too. As if she didn't know anything sometimes. I wondered when he would see that she was almost grown, too. But I guess it was just brotherly affection.

We walked into town separately so not to be noticed that much by the people. I was with Perl, her mother, and Korah. Tsuli held her mother's hand and Temmen was in Teamalie's arms. We were on the side of the street, walking on a wooden walkway.

    I saw a woman walking our way up ahead. Her head was high and she had a fast, light, stride. Another Thasfaen.

    As she approached Tsuli ran up to her, calling, "Gramma! Gramma!"

    She smiled, knelt, and held out her arms wide, "Hey there, Tsuli, oh!" she said as he ran into her, making her tip over. She chuckled, "My, how you've grown!"

    "Ma, how've yeh been?" Korah asked, helping her up, then hugged her.

    "Just fine, although it's been quiet without the boys runnin' 'round."

    "How's Papa?"

    "Stubborn's always."

    Korah chortled, "I'm not surprised." She pointed to us, "Yeh remember Teamalie, and Perl, her daughter. She's been helpin' me with the children." She turned to me, "And this's Eleny, a new follower of Elyon, and her wixes, she's been travelin' with us for a while now."

    We all shook the Thasfaen's hands as she said, "My name's Zerah, it's lovely to meet yeh all." She turned back to Korah, "Let's go to tha house, the men's already there, eatin' my blueberry pie. If you wanna a piece, we'd better hurry before it's a gone."

We followed her down the road, turning down different streets. When we reached a house that was two stories high, we went inside.

Just like Zerah said with her funny accent, there was pie. Well, half of it, hence the men moaning that they ate too much.

Soon we had dinner and were in the sitting room.

Korah's father, Lorny, was a sea captain, plump and joyful, cracking jokes all the time. I liked him, he was hilarious.

"Me no understand people humor."

Noctua was on my arm, Little Blue in my lap. My arm was now healed, the one Noctua was on, and was as healthy as it was before, with a fading scar.

"It looks a lot better."

I glanced to see Perl looking down at me. "Yep, almost completely gone."

She nodded.

Zerah walked up, "Do yeh wanna to see where yeh two sleep tonight?"

"Sure," we replied.

"Follow me." She walked down a hallway

and we followed.

We reached a door that revealed two beds. "You can come to tha kitchen any time in the mornin', I'll be up." She said, "If you need anythin' tonight, yer parents are tha next door down." At that she briskly walked back out and closed the door.

Perl sat on a bed, "Korah's parents have, like, fifteen rooms, like this one, throughout the house."

"Whoa."

"I know, right? A lot of rooms for a lot of kids, Korah has many brothers and sisters who've moved out." Her feet swung back and forth.

I went to the window and looked out. It was a perfect view of the full moon and waves crashing against the rocks. I took a deep breath of the salty air. Sighing, I scratched Little Blue's chest.

"It very beautiful."

Yes, it is beautiful.

"Me love the moon, me mother speak of moon a lot." Noctua hopped down, landing on the sil.

What was your mother's bird form?

She looked down and thought a moment. *"Me think it was a very small owl kind, me was still little, so me no know exactly what."*

I nodded, smoothing her feathers.

TWENTY ONE

Zerah's Advice

The street was busier than it was yesterday, I tried not to lose sight of the women I was following in the large crowd.

We were going to have tea with some of Zerah's friends. I packed some food for Little Blue, I had no idea how long this would be.

For breakfast we had flat cakes with honey, and milk or coffee on the side. Zerah gave Little Blue some pan eggs, for which I was grateful, and he absolutely loved it.

Before long we were on our way, walking through the streets of River Port. Every now and then I would catch a glimpse of the dark blue water, ships on the horizon.

I suddenly wished Alex was with me as I walked down the street.

"Are you nervous?"

I turned to see Perl walk up beside me.

"Yeah, I guess. I mean, this would be the first time to do this sort of thing." I smoothed Noctua's feathers.

Perl nodded, "I grew up doing this, so I'm kind of used to it. If you need any help with these talkative ladies, just get me."

"I'm glad *you* feel comfortable doing this."

She shrugged and kept walking.

After a while we finally reached another large house. Zerah knocked on the door.

A round woman with rosy cheeks welcomed us in, "Come on in, come on in! So nice to see yeh again Korah, it's been a long while." They hugged, and we followed her into the living room. Seven other Thasfaens were sitting on the sofas around a table. They all greeted Zerah and Korah, smiling at the children.

When everyone was seated, Noctua, Little Blue, and I in a corner, when the round woman, whose name was Lona, started speaking.

"Ladies, ladies! May I have yer attention please!"

The women quieted and looked at her.

"Thank you. Now. First we're gonna to listen to what Korah an' her family, along with the Bends, have done since they've been'ere last. Then we'll begin our meetin'." She motioned for Korah to speak.

Then Korah began, "First of all, it's wonderful seein' you all again. So far, we've brought many to Elyon." They smiled and cheered.

When they quieted down again, she and Teamalie went back and forth, telling them all what they had done this year.

I quietly listened and watched little Temmen and Little Blue play with each other. I looked over and saw Perl's bored face.

Eleny Nil to Perlelia Bend.

"Welcome." She looked at me.

You've been to a lot of these, right?

"Yes."

You seem pretty bored.

She shrugged. *"You could say that."*

Well, since you've been like this before, you should know how to pass the time.

"What do you mean?"

I mean I'm bored, too. I already know all of what they're talking about. What do you normally do in places like this?

"Hmm, give me a second."

I looked back at the wixen and baby, but kept my connection with Perl open. Soon she connected again.

"How about we could state our favorite THINGS!"

Sounds good to me.

She rolled her eyes. *"I was being sarcastic."*

Well, too bad. What's your favorite colors?

She rolled her eyes again, but I saw the corners of her mouth twitch. *"Fine, I like green and the blue of the sky."*

A pause.

She finally mind groaned. *"Eleny, what are your favorite colors?"*

I grinned. *Light blue and beige.*

"Nice."

Okay, what is your favorite thing to do with Timna?

"You're quick at this."

Why thank you. Answer the question.

She mind groaned again. *"Oh, that's actually really hard, there are so many things!"*

Then just say what you do most with her that you love.

"Well, I love to do tricks with her, like how

sometimes I lead her with my hand as she, in bird form, spins around me."

That sounds amazing.

"We'll have to show you sometime. What about you?"

I thought a minute. *I love it when Noctua starts to preen me, or when I smooth her feathers. She does this cute little thing, her eyes close and she does a soft whistle.*

"Okay, now my turn to ask the question. What is... your favorite memory?"

I paused. I thought of Grandmother, cuddling up with me on a cold season day. Of my father, telling me stories.

To be honest, I'm not sure. What about you?

"Yeah, same here. There are so many. Not the best question I guess."

We continued our little game until the meeting was over. Tomorrow we were going to cook and bake for the day, then give the food to some families who needed help.

I had no idea what I was going to be doing, I guess I would have to just stick with one person and do what they were doing.

I yawned and looked up at the ceiling.

Something had woken me up, but I wasn't really sure what. It was something.

Something else, far away.

Something that didn't feel right.

The feeling vanished from my mind when I heard Noctua coo at my neck. I glanced down at Little Blue, who was curled under my arm.

Trying not to disturb each of the wixes, I turned to look across the room. Perl and Timna were curled up in their blankets, only Perl's head was visible, while her bonded's long tail was poking out from underneath.

I slipped out from my quilt and opened the door. Before I stepped through, there was a whoosh and two grabs to my shoulders.

I knew that Noctua, the silent flier, was supposed to be teaching the young wixen how to be quieter in his flight. But his feathers weren't the best kind for that talent, so I didn't blame her completely.

I smiled up at them. *Good morning.*

"*Good morning.*" Noctua started preening my hair.

Do you want to go have some breakfast?

"*Yes, me tell Little Blue.*"

A moment later he was off, flying down the

hall in the direction of the kitchen. It took a minute for me to catch up to him, and when we stepped into the large room, he already had a plate in front of him that held some sausage. Zerah was over the stove, stirring the eggs.

I looked back at Little Blue, "Thanks for feeding him."

She glanced up at me, "I'm use' to it, so it's fine."

"Used to it?"

"Well, I guess it's been a while." She looked back at me, "Korah raised'er yellow warbler wix, and I helped very much. She's only twelve at this time, so she'd needed as much help as she could get," she smiled.

Realization hit me, "Wait, what's your last name?"

Her face was puzzled, "Johm."

I sucked in a breath and took out the wix book, turned to the section about wixen, and pointed at her name. "Did *you* write this?"

"Yep. A writer came to me and asked about wixen, this's what he must've used tha infermation fer." She looked closer at the paper, "That's definitely my name, and what I'd told'im."

"Do you think you could give me some tips?

As you've seen, I've been taking care of him." I pointed at Little Blue.

Her eyebrows furrowed and she stirred the egg some more, then took the pan off the stove. She then took two plates, put some of the food on them, and gave one to me. "I'll try to 'elp, but like I said in tha book, it's difficult."

I nodded, "I think I know that already. You have no idea, nor does anyone else, how much mischief he's made."

"Oh, I'm afraid that I do. Petechia was really energetic. Much more so than this calm one," she gestured to Little Blue.

I glanced at the bright blue wixen, "He's calm compared to Petechia?"

"At this age, yeah."

"Whoa, you must have been patient. I can barely keep from going crazy with all of his antics to try and get attention. Noctua is wonderful, me and her get along well. Don't we?" I looked at Noctua.

"Yes, we do."

"Well, that's 'cause Elyon chose for you two to be 'gether," Zerah said. "He knew you'd be perfect for each other."

I nodded as she continued, "Also, you can't

talk to Little Blue directly, so that dudn't help much either. Korah couldn't talk to Petechia until she's able to transform, a year later! And I never'd had a wix, so it's all by experience. My daughter hadn't wanted the wixen as a bonded when she first found'er, she'd been planning on lettin' the yellow creature go when she was old enough. Korah was very surprised when Chia stayed and became'er bonded. And now I'm very thankful Elyon brought the wix to us. Now the two've been bonded for over fifteen years."

"Whoa, so are you saying Little Blue will probably become my second bonded?" I wasn't sure how I felt about that.

"There's no tellin', I've a friend who cared for a wixen for a year, an' he was never bonded to it. One day the wix went into the forest and he never saw it again! The man was devastated."

"Hmm." Would *I want a second bonded? I just really wanted to help Little Blue until he was old enough to live by himself. I guess it would be pretty amazing.*

I ate a bite of egg, savoring the flavor. I gave a piece to Noctua and she gobbled it up.

Soon everyone was up and around, eating breakfast in the dining room.

I sat down by Alex, "Good morning, Alex."

He grinned back, "Good morning, Eleny."

I continued drinking my coffee as everybody visited.

"So, where's you goin' to next? Kulan?"

My ears perked up and I looked down the table. Lorny was talking to Grimblon.

Grimblon nodded at him, "Yes, Kulan, then Meent."

The Thasfaen's frown effected his whole face, making his cheeks sag. "Oh."

"Lorny..." Grimblon warned, "What's wrong?"

"It's just that, what I hears from Meent idn't good news. A merchant came by few days 'go and said that theys gone through one o' those raids."

Now Grimblon was frowning. "Then we will help them all we can when we get there."

Wait, Meent? But, that's where Palana went! Oh, I hope she's alright!

"Me too." Noctua was perched on the back of my chair. Even though Noctua hadn't met her, she knew Palana by hearing my thoughts. At first I was wary of it, but I was now comfortable with her knowing about my life with just her mind linked to mine.

"Mother when are we meeting with the

others?" Perl asked, from across the table.

Teamalie looked at Perl, but Zerah got to her first, "We're gonna cook until noon first, then 'ave lunch with tha ladies back at Lona's. After that we're gonna go give the food to the poor families and children, all the while teaching'em of Elyon."

Perl nodded.

"How 'bout we start now?" Zerah glanced at Teamalie, "We could get a lot cooked if we do."

"That's a good idea," Teamalie thought, then turned to Perl and I, "Are you two helping?"

I nodded, "I know how to bake a few things."

"Sure," Perl said at the same time.

"Yow!" Zerah cried, jumping back from the pan, "Gee, that burned my hand real good."

We were in the kitchen and had already baked an apple pie and a blueberry pie, and chicken was boiling in a pot. Now Zerah was pulling a cherry pie out of oven, burning her hand because she forgot the hot pad for the third time.

Each time Perl and I stifled chortling and I even heard Noctua hoo and hoot sometimes.

"She is clumsy."

I glanced at Noctua, who was perched on

the window-sill with Little Blue.

You can say that again.

Teamalie gestured to the bowl full of water she had filled for Zerah's hand, "Maybe you should remind yourself of the tools you have," she said ruefully.

"I'll remember next time," Zerah put her hand in the bowl of water again, "After the chicken's done, we'll start heading to Lona's."

And that's what we did. We were welcomed the same way we were the day before and had a light meal.

After that, we carried all the food in baskets and hit the road to down town. We probably looked odd, a bunch of women walking in the middle of the street holding bags and baskets.

Zerah was walking next to Teamalie and I. "So," I said, directing my voice to Zerah, "how often do you do this?"

She glanced at me, "Twice a week we meet, once fer sewin' and knittin' blankets or clothes, tha other we meet like we did yesterday, tha next day bringin' food fer tha people. Pretty soon we'll spit up in smaller groups, goin' to separate places."

"That's great, not many people would put

themselves out of there way for others."

"Yes, the world isn't like it once was," she frowned.

TWENTY TWO

Visiting and Giving

Hi there sweetheart, how are yeh today?" Korah knelt down and rubbed the girl's shoulder.

She didn't speak, or wear a smile.

Her mother, who seemed a little over middle-aged, came out of the small house and smiled, "Hello, it's been a while since you've come out here with yer mother."

"We've been travelin' all over and are stoppin' by for a week." Korah stood back up and gave the woman a hug, "How're you doin'?"

She gave a weak smile, "Just survivin'."

Korah, Temmen in her arms, and Zerah followed her into the little house and I stayed out on the steps with the girl. She looked about eight years, she had straight brown hair, and big violet eyes. She just sat there, looking down at the grass, not even noticing the wixes on my shoulders.

Children were running around the house, playing games in the dirt, or climbing the now bare trees, some even just stared at Little Blue and Noctua from a distance.

Like Zerah said earlier that day, we split up into smaller groups. Perl went with her mother, who was watching Tsuli, and another lady and I went with Korah and Zerah.

I decided to go inside, hearing the girl's soft footsteps behind me.

Sauntering in, I took notice of the dirt covered floor, muddy shoes, and, at least I thought, all kinds of makeshift toys in the corners of the rooms.

The women were sitting on some old, dusty, sofas in the sitting room.

I sat on a stool and listened to the conversation for a minute until the woman noticed her daughter.

"Come'ere darlin'," the woman said, calling

the girl to her.

The shy little one shuffled over.

"Kaddie hasn't spoken but a few words since'er father died," the Thasfaen sighed, lifting her daughter onto her lap.

"Pury, I know it was hard on yeh last cold season, since'is death," Zerah said, "But please, if yeh need anythin' at all, just call on me."

She nodded and combed her fingers through her daughter's hair.

"She sad."

I glanced at Noctua. *The mother?*

"She sad, but I mean the girl. She even sadder."

I changed my gaze. *She does look depressed. She must have really loved her father.*

"Yes."

"The older girls watches over the littles while I'm out workin' at the tailer's." Pury sighed, she seemed to sigh often, "My oldest son, Juhn, wanna's to start workin' at tha mill soon, so that'll be helpin' a lot."

"Well, we brought some blankets," Zerah piped up, "we hope you'll accept'em." She held them out for Pury.

Kaddie touched the soft fabric as Pury took them. "Thank yeh." she set them on a chair and stood up, "Let'sa go outside and enjoy tha warm day, this's bound to be one o' tha last this year."

We went back outside, I strode over to a large rock and sat. Little Blue hopped off and laid down beside me. Sighing, I watched the children play.

I was unaware of the quiet child until Little Blue started chirping. Turning my gaze I saw Kaddie petting his head, something was in her hand, but I couldn't see what.

"Do you like him?"

She nodded.

"What do you have there?"

She looked down and opened her fingers. In the palm of her hand was a little lizard. It's arm was bent in a weird way, and it's head had a scratch.

"Oh no, what happened to it?"

Kaddie frowned and pointed at one of the little boys who was a little taller than her.

"Oh. Can I hold it?"

She pursed her lips and finally nodded, handing me the little green creature.

I held it, it barely weighed anything. I laid my the other hand on it's back. *Elyon imi kuzon.* My finger tips lit. A few more moments later I took my hand off and showed Kaddie.

She gasped and took the little lizard, it's arm was in better condition and all that was left of the scratch was a thin scar.

Kaddie petted it's smooth green back. She looked up at me with wide pupils and smiled.

I took that as a thank you. "But you can't tell anyone about this, okay?"

She nodded.

I turned my gaze back to the children playing, a few minutes later I gathered my courage, I asked quietly, "Do you miss your father?"

She barely flinched, but I saw it, then she nodded again, slower this time.

"You know, I lost my mother."

She jerked her head up and looked at me, "You did?"

Surprised at her speaking, I nodded, "Yes, soon after I was born. I didn't even know her."

Kaddie frowned, "Oh."

After a pause I asked, "You loved your father very much didn't you?"

A quiet "Yes" came from those small lips.

"My father went missing when I was a little younger than you, and I loved him dearly. His big hands-"

"Warm hugs-" she gave a little smile.

"Loud laugh-"

"Funny jokes," she giggled, "I miss'im a whole lot."

"I'm sure you do," I softly patted her back.

She then had a far away look in her eyes, "Yeh know, he's used to take me along fishin' with'im an' my brothers, even when they didn't wanna me to."

"I bet he was amazing."

She sniffed again, "Yeah, he was. He called me'is little lass."

Another pause.

"Do you know who Elyon is?"

It took a few moments before she answered, "Well, Ma talks of Him sometimes. But I don't really know who He is."

"He is our Father, he created you and me. He watches over us and is with us at all times. He loves us."

"But my Pa died." Her eyebrows furrowed.

Trying to figure out a way to explain, I bit my lip. "Yes, but that was your father here in Iyim. You have another Father up in the heavens. He has always been. He created this world. He cares for you, me, your Ma, your Pa, your brothers and sisters, everybody!"

"He does?" A tiny smile appeared on her face.

"Yes, and He is watching you and me right now, talking about Him."

She looked up at the sky and smiled even bigger, "He is?"

I grinned, "Yes, He is."

"Whoa, that's 'mazing!"

"He wants you to talk to him, to tell Him your worries."

Her smiled disappeared and she looked back down, "If He watches ever'body, He don't have no time fer me."

I lifted her chin to look at me, "He loves everyone. He loves *you* Kaddie. He has time for you just like He has time for everyone else."

Without warning, she wrapped her arms around my torso and squeezed. I closed my eyes and squeezed back.

After the lovely moment passed, Kaddie leaned into me and asked, "So I can talk to Elyon anytime? He doesn't mind?"

"Kaddie, He *wants* you to talk to Him. But you know what?"

"What?"

I gazed down at her. "Your mother wants you to talk to her too. She loves you, Kaddie."

"I know." She smiled, hopping off the rock. She ran to her mother, wrapped her arms around her mother's neck, and said, "Ma!"

I walked over, and couldn't explain how much love was showing on the Thasfaen's face. Tears were streaming down her face as she embraced the little girl.

Both Zerah and Korah looked at me, then at the girl, then back at me.

My cheeks heated under all three of the women's stares.

I sat in the grass and started to pick it. Their gazes were on me until Korah suggested that they hand out the mittens they brought for the children.

The rest of the time we were there, everything was a blur. Little Blue was playing with the boys, Noctua was on my shoulder. Once we called the, I don't know how many, children over, all around was calling, shouting, or just plain screaming. We almost didn't have enough mittens, but we found one last pair for the last boy.

We then had the lunch we brought in the baskets, I didn't get one bite. Children, of all ages, got their fill by scrambling for every piece of food they could grab.

Soon we were on our way back to the Johm's home. When we got back we found no one there. All three of us went to our rooms.

"*Me just tired from watching!*" Noctua hopped off my shoulder, onto the bed.

I laid down beside her and yawned. *Then that means I'm even more tired than you. I was the one who handed out those mittens. And don't forget that food! I've never seen so many fingers at one time in my life!*

I covered myself with the light blanket on top of the quilt and laid my head down. *Please wake me when the others arrive.*

"*Me will try, but me might not be awake when they do.*"

I was already drifting off to sleep.

"Goodness, you must have done much today."

I sat up quickly, making my head spin.

Perl was sitting on her bed.

I thumped back down on my pillow, "Many many children, many more mouths to feed. Ten times more fingers, grabbing for everything."

She giggled at my rhyme, a sound I hadn't heard from her in a while. "You went to Pury's, did you?" she inquired.

"Yes."

She giggled again, "Then I understand why you're lying down in bed."

Little Blue lifted his practically glowing blue head and hopped off the bed to greet Perl. She scratched behind his ear and he chirped at her. "He must be some kind of perch bird, from how much he tweets. Prey birds caw or screech, he just whistles and chirps."

"Yes, I think he might be, too," I said, "I wonder if there's a book of birds Raeya packed me."

Perl sat by me as I took the box out of my pocket and whispered, "Library," and it opened up to the large book cabinet, sitting on the floor.

I scanned the names, stopping at a four-inches thick book that said "Ave of Iyim" and grabbed it. I started at the contents of the book and it was separated into a three groups, prey birds, perch birds, water birds.

I turned the pages to perch birds. It showed a painting of the bird next to the description of it. All colors, from red to blue and black to white.

I scoured every page that had a speck of blue, but there were so many birds that had that shade, I decided that we would just have to find out when the time came.

"Hmm, I just had a thought," Perl said, staring at the ceiling.

As I put the book away, I asked, "What?"

She looked down at me, "How do the wixes know what kind of bird form they have when they transform?"

I shrugged, "I'll ask, maybe you could ask Timna," I referred to the white, black, and salmon bird sitting on the 'sil. I then smoothed Noctua's feathers as she slept. She twitched, then groggily stood, flapped her wings, and perched on my shoulder.

"Hmm?"

Perl and I were wondering how you learned of your bird form's name.

She stared at Perl and I, blinking, seeming to try to know how to explain. *"It strange. Me tell you from beginning.*

"*When me almost full grown, me have strange feeling inside me. Me stand, and light go around me. When me open my eyes, everything around me bigger! Me unfold my wings, and they a similar, but different shape! Then, somehow me knew that me a barn owl wix. When my father get home from hunting, he sees me and tells me how to turn back to wix form. Soon after I left on my own and I say good bye."*

Whoa.

"Yep."

I sat back and gazed at Little Blue for a minute.

"So, what did Noctua say?" Perl asked.

I told her, and she agreed, "Yes, that's what Timna said, apart from her father. Timna said good bye to both her mother and father when she left."

I nodded.

"We're going to the tavern for dinner," Teamalie stepped in, "Everyone is a little worn out from today and don't want to cook."

I laughed, "Yeah, we've done many things today."

She smiled back, "Meet us in the sitting room in half an hour." She stepped back out.

Yawning, I asked Perl, "Have you been to the tavern here?"

"Yes, the cook is a friend of my father's. He's a great cook. His specialties are fish, of course. Living at a port when most of the population are fisherman or shrimpers, that's really all you have to eat, apart from the seaweed."

She made a face, "Don't try the seaweed they serve here, it only tastes like raw fish, trust me, I've learned the hard way." Then she smiled again, "Although, if you ever visit Portum, a port in the north-west corner of Iyim, definitely try the seaweed there. It's a different type, and they season and bake it. Then it's all crunchy, like bacon. It's so delicious." She licked her lips.

My stomach growled and Little Blue growled back, I laughed, "All this talk of food is making me hungry."

Perl giggled when her stomach made a weird noise, "Same here."

"Alexovin Hendruton to Eleny Nil."

I jumped when the voice came. *Welcome. What, Alex?*

No answer.

Alex?

A frigid coldness came, but still no answer. "Eleny? Eleny!"

I lost connection and turned to Perl, "Yes?"

Her eyes were wide, "It's just that, you looked as though something happened. Your eyes were half way open, and you were staring like you were dead. It just scared me."

"Oh, that's what I must look like when I'm mindvoicing."

Perl gave a sigh of relief, "Whew. Who were you talking to?"

"I—" I paused. "I don't know. Alex asked permission, but when I welcomed him, he didn't answer."

Noctua, did you feel anything?

"Me don't know, it happen so fast! All me felt was super cold."

Me, too.

I stood, "I need to go see if he's alright." I ran out, sending Noctua ahead of me.

He might be getting ready to leave for the tavern, maybe he's in his room. But where is it?

"Me don't know, but me feel his presence, it is close."

I stopped. I felt it too.

Turning around, we headed toward his mind. I again stopped, this time at a door.

I knocked, the door handle jiggled.

The door opened, "What?"

TWENTY THREE

Something Strange

Dark shadows were beneath his eyes, the normal color of them, pale green, was now more of a gray.

I swallowed and looked up at Alex, "You asked me permission, but when I welcomed you, you didn't answer."

His eyebrows furrowed and the worry line appeared, "I didn't ask."

I stood, at a loss for words.

He glanced down the hall, then back at me, "I'll be down in a minute." He closed the door.

I frowned. *That was weird. He didn't know he asked.*

"Yes, strange."

I walked to the sitting room, Little Blue was perched atop Perl's shoulder. His gaze turned up and with a few flaps of his wings, he was on my shoulder.

The Grimblon and Teamalie were waiting in the hall.

"Are you ready girls?" Teamalie asked.

"Yes," we both answered.

"Good."

"Where's Alex?" Grimblon called. "Is he coming?"

"Yes, I'm here, let's go!" Alex stepped in.

We followed Grimblon out the door, the sun was almost setting.

On the walk there, I kept an eye on Alex, walking only a few feet away from him. I knew he could take care of himself, but after earlier I was a little worried about him.

We finally made it to the tavern, which was a two story building. The inn was on top, the tavern on bottom.

Inside people, Thasfaens and Jinde, crowded around round wooden tables. Laughing and conversations buzzed, the smell of salty food filled my nostrils.

A girl that looked to be in her early twenties walked up, "Can I help yeh?"

"Yes, we need a table." Grimblon said, "I would also like to talk with the cook."

She nodded, "All righty, follow me." She showed us to a table and when we were seated she spoke to Grimblon, "I'll go get tha cook, but he's a mighty busy right now, so no promises he'll come."

"Just tell him the Bends are here," Grimblon responded.

She nodded and walked around the tables, through a swing door.

Thin wooden board menus were on the table, I grabbed one. "Is the shrimp plate good?"

Teamalie nodded, "Yes, I've had it."

"What comes on it?"

Her finger tapped the table, "Boiled shrimp, salad, and a slice of bread. The shrimp isn't just boiled, though. It has delicious spices. You should try it."

"I think I will," I set the board back down on

the table.

"What is simp?"

Noctua was on my shoulder, Little Blue beside me on the floor.

A creature that lives in the ocean. And it's SH-rimp.

"Can me try simp?"

I rolled my eyes and smiled. *Of course you can.*

A large Thasfaen walked up, his apron was covered in stains from food. "Why, if it isn't Grimblon Bend!"

Grimblon stood and shook the man's hand, "Good to see you again, Werrid. How's the wife?"

"Oh, she's just fine! We're gonna have a third pretty soon." He grinned.

"Well then congratulations!" Grimblon clapped the man's shoulder.

"Yep, Tersy's hopin' fer a girl this time. I am, too, although I love my boys, even if they get into trouble," He laughed. "So, yeh stayin' for how long this time?"

"Oh, about another week. We wanted to stop by and have some dinner after a day of work. Teamalie and the girls here went to give out food down town. Alex and I had a meeting today and we're going down town tomorrow."

"Well then, dinner's on me."

"Werrid, you don't have to do—"

"Yep I do. Yeh order whatever yeh want."

Grimblon glanced at Teamalie and smiled.

"Now, I've to get back to tha kitchen. I'll see to it that yeh get yer food." He strode back across the room, through the swing door. Soon the woman came back and we ordered.

I glanced at Alex, he wasn't focused on Grimblon and Teamalie's conversation. His eyes were closed and his face was strained, no one seemed to notice. I decided to talk to him.

Eleny Nil to Alexovin Hendruton.

His face expression didn't change. I tried again.

Eleny Nil to Alexovin Hendruton.

Still no answer, just the frigidness.

Noctua, what do you think?

"Me never see something like this before. But me no like it."

Maybe he just doesn't want to talk to me. Or maybe he has a headache.

Since he didn't answer my mindvoicing, I decided to do something else. "So Alex, what all have you done today?"

He didn't move.

"Alex?"

Grimblon noticed me and frowned, "He's been doing that all day. Ever since this morning."

"What did you do this morning?"

"We went to the men's meeting."

"Hmm." I knew something was wrong, but I couldn't figure it out. I poked his arm.

His eyes opened, but his face didn't relax. "What?"

"Are you alright?"

He looked at me, then down at the table, "Just a headache."

I didn't know what to think. It didn't seem like it was just a headache.

I whispered to Teamalie that I was going to the privy, and she pointed down a hall. I went inside the little room and shut the door behind me. I then took out my box and whispered 'cold box and hot box'. It unfolded.

I had made some tea in bottles ahead of time for times like this. There was mint, chamomile, thyme, lemon balm, and a few others.

I grabbed the mint and poured it in a mug. I then put it in the hot box, closing the door. After a minute I opened it back up, the tea was steaming.

I grinned. I'd never used the hot box before, never needed to, so I was glad it worked.

I opened the door and walked back to the table. I gave the mug to Alex and smiled, "Some mint tea for the headache."

He looked suspiciously at it and said sharply, "No thanks."

"Oh," I looked down at my lap, hurt by his cold tone towards me.

Did I do something wrong? Did it have to do with my answer? I didn't actually say no. I just said I needed to think.

Noctua noticed my frown and nudged my cheek with her head.

Mr. Werrid came out the swing door with a tray of food. He made his way to our table and served it. "Come an' say goodbye before ya leave."

"We will, friend."

He smiled and walked back to the kitchen.

Mm. This looks good.

The plate, like Teamalie explained, had shrimp covered in orange and red spices. The bread slice was warm and fresh. The salad, well, let's just say it wasn't as I hoped. The leaves were turning brown, and the little red tomatoes had dents.

I glanced around, no one was looking my way. I touched the salad with my index finger. The finger lit up and the salad turned bright green, the tomatoes' dents gone. I grinned and put on salt and pepper.

Maybe it's a little selfish for using my gift just for myself, but it is my gift so oh well. Huh, I don't feel tired. Maybe that's something I won't find in a book. When I heal plants, it doesn't take as much energy.

Noctua hopped from one foot to the other. *"Now me try simp?"*

Yes.

I grabbed a piece and gave it to Little Blue, then to her. They gobbled it up.

"Mm, that really, very good!"

I took a bite. *Mm, you're right.*

My, or should I say *our*, food was gone in a matter of minutes.

Grimblon stood, "I'll go say goodbye to Werrid, I'll meet you on the porch." He walked off.

Teamalie stood and sighed, "That was delicious. Let's go."

We followed her out the door and waited. The sun was about to disappear, only a sliver of orange left.

Ten minutes later Grimblon stepped out, then we were back on the road.

"Ready for bed?"
Teamalie was checking on Perl and I before she went to bed herself. I liked how caring Teamalie was of her daughter.
"Yes Mother," said Perl.
"Alright, good night girls."
"Good night, Mother!"
Perl acted annoyed at her loving mother.
Which annoyed me.
Which made Noctua anxious.
Which made Little Blue restless.
Which made him reckless and start digging in the blankets.
Which made me start getting a little aggravated.
Do you see where I'm going with this?
Anyway, after we got home, I visited in the sitting room for a while, drank some coffee, went to our room, talked with Perl, got ready for bed, and here I am, lying down in bed.
"Time for sleep!" My body tells me.
But then my brain argues with my arms and legs, "No! There's too much to think about! Like

why has Alex started acting weird? Does it have to do with us being awkward with each other since he said he was beginning to care for me? Why do I not spend so much energy on plants when I heal them? How do I get Little Blue to listen? He's like a little newborn puppy that needs to be taken care of every ten minutes! Is Palana alright? Is she safe? Did something happen to her? I don't know her that well, it's not like we're family or something. But I still worry for her!"

Then my sense kicks in.

Clear up brain! Sleep! You need rest after today! Elyon please *clear my mind.*

I sat up, Noctua was curled up at my waist, Little Blue at my feet. Perl was asleep under her covers.

Since my bed was under the window, I reached over and grabbed the curtain. The full moon shined through and lit my bed, so I unfolded my box to the library. I took out Elyon's Word then opened it in the middle and started reading.

'*I will both lay down peacefully and sleep. For only thou, oh Elyon, makest me dwell in safety.*'

I turned a few pages.

'*I will love thee, oh Elyon, my strength. Elyon is my rock, fortress, and deliverer. My God, my strength, in whom I trust. My shield and salvation, my high tower. I will call upon Elyon, who is worthy to be praised, so shall I be saved.'*

I yawned and turned another few pages. The words calmed my nerves, so I started reading slower.

'Elyon is my light and my salvation, whom shall I fear? Elyon is the strength of my life, of whom shall I be afraid?'

'Unto thee, oh Elyon, we give thanks, unto thee we do give thanks. For thy wondrous works declare thy name is near. . .'

Sleep overtook.

TWENTY FOUR

Goodbyes and more Strangeness

Good mornin', Eleny," said Zerah.

Zerah, like the all the other mornings that we'd been there, fed Little Blue some breakfast.

Yesterday it was eggs, today it was sausage.

The past week it had been busy. Busy. Busy. And busy.

We served food, made blankets, had meetings, sewed clothes, and taught people of Elyon. Of course whenever Teamalie was teaching about Him, I was listening and learning, too.

We were leaving for Kulon today. No one was up yet, but it was early, the sun had just risen.

I enjoyed having my mornings with Zerah. She taught me how to care for Little Blue, and if I was early enough, I helped her cook breakfast, like I was doing right now. "Good morning Zerah. Can I help with anything?"

"Of course, yeh can fry these eggs." She pointed to a bowl full of eggs, then to a pan, "Yeh can use that."

"Got it." I cracked the eggs on the rim of the pan and poured it in. "How do you wake up in the morning almost every day and fix food for so many people?"

She chuckled, "When yeh've got little ones wakin' yeh up, askin' fer food before the sun comes, yeh get used to it. I'd twelve children that I had to feed. To cook that much food takes a time to make. Korah was one of the youngest. I'd a kid in the house up until this past year, when he got married." She chuckled again, "And boy, was he a handful."

I grinned at how you could tell how much she loved her children.

"So yeh ready fer tha trip today?"

I shrugged, "Yeah, I guess. Little Blue has

been growing these past weeks, he'll be flying more than sitting with me on Noctua's back. He can't even sit on my shoulder anymore, being half the size of Noctua while she's in wix form."

Zerah flipped a flat cake and nodded, "How much longer do yeh think it is 'til he can change into a bird?"

My eyebrows furrowed as I counted, "Sometime in the next moon. He's grown rapidly."

"Yep, once they get growin' fast they don't stop 'til they're done."

I flipped an egg and continued to crack, pour, salt, and flip until all of them were fried.

I was putting the last egg on a plate when everyone started getting up. The kitchen and dining room were soon full of people.

"We'll be leaving soon after breakfast everyone!" Grimblon announced, standing so that every person in the room could hear, "So everybody needs to be packed and ready out in the back in an hour."

"Bye Zerah, I'll miss our talks. Thank you for all you've taught me." We embraced.

"Me too, I thank Elyon we met." She stepped back, holding my hands. "G'bye, have a safe trip."

I jumped up on Noctua and smoothed her soft-feathered neck. I searched around and found Little Blue's bright blue head. He was pawing at Corvus' tail like a cat as it swished back and forth. Corvus lifted it and hit Little Blue across the head. Little Blue yelped and ran away.

I suppressed a laugh. Noctua did not.

She started hooting and hooing like crazy.

Noctua?

"Hoo hoo hoo! You see what Corvus did to little wixen? He had coming!"

Noctua?

"Hoo hoo hoo!"

Noctua! I slapped the wix's side.

"Oh, what?"

Get Little Blue over here and ask if he'll be riding at first.

She called him by screeching her screech, except it was twice as loud while in wix form. Every person in the back yard, including the Bends, Johms, and Rambeys, all jumped, yelped, or gasped, eyeballing Noctua.

NOCTUA!

Noctua took a step back and shrunk, similar to when she was in owl form. Little Blue walked up slowly to Noctua, head down.

Noctua. . . you okay?

"Yes, me just not mean to do it that loud. Me sorry."

I patted her side, "Uh, heh, sorry everyone, she didn't mean to do it that loud."

They then went back to there goodbyes.

"Can we go now?"

Yes, but tell Little Blue to get up here.

"Okay."

Little Blue hopped up in my lap, he barely fit, and we waited until all were on their wixes and were ready to fly.

Grimblon gave the call and we were off the ground in a blur.

Once we were high enough and the wixes were able to flap less and soar instead, Little Blue flew beside us.

Grimblon and Corvus were at point, then it went to Teamalie, who was holding Tsuli, Perl and Timna, then to Korah and Temmen, Amon and Amalek, and me.

Goodness, that's a lot of people. How long will we be traveling before we reach Kulan?

Eleny Nil to Alexovin Hendruton.

No answer, just a weird frigid cold. He was

blocking me. My chest sagged. Why was he blocking me? His mind was stronger than mine at blocking, so I couldn't break through and read his mind.

I searched and found him flying at the back. I tried again but failed. I searched for Perl instead.

Eleny Nil to Perlelia Bend.

"Oh, uh, uh, welcome! Sorry, forgot what to say right then. What's up?"

The sky and us.

I felt her eye roll. "Eleny, well duh!"

I'm teasing. I was just wondering how long It'll take to reach Kulan.

"Um, last time it took. . . I think three days and two nights. So we'll travel today, stop for lunch, then stop to sleep. Then we'll do that again tomorrow, the next day arriving at Kulan."

Thank you.

"You're welcome."

I was about to cut the connection but Perl caught me.

"Wait, would you like to keep talking?"

I smiled. *Sure, about what?*

"Anything. Like, why is Alex acting like this? He hasn't ever ignored me like he has in the past few days. I'm just a little worried. And well, he's always been the sarcastic type and sometimes distant, but never ignore me completely. And it's weird because it's like you and I are the only ones that are noticing."

I frowned. *I can't really answer you. I think something's wrong, but I can't seem to figure it out. I've tried mindvoicing him, but it's like talking to a wall.*

She sighed. *"Oh well."*

So where are we going to stay when we get to Kulon?

"At an inn. You and I will probably be sharing a room with Mother and Korah, and of course Tsuli and Temmen. Father and Alex will share a room with Amon and Amalek. That way it saves money, only renting two rooms."

Makes sense.

She sighed again.

What?

"Just a little tired. Didn't sleep well. And I think a headache's coming on."

Oh. I can give you some mint tea when we land for lunch.

"Thank you, that would help a lot."

We stayed silent for a while until I decided to cut the connection.

When the sun was high Grimblon made the

signal to land. We descended, following him to a grassy green field. Every one was busy getting their lunches.

Hmm, what should I have for lunch? I dug my folding box out of my coat pocket and said 'Cold box. Hot box. Blankets'. It unfolded to the drawer with the cold and hot boxes on the side. I took out a blanket and laid it on the ground, then opened the cold box.

There were apples, pears, some biscuits from Zerah's kitchen, and old cheese that was growing mold.

Ew. New rule. Go through cold box more often. I threw it out into a field.

"Yes ew, that disgusting!" Noctua put her head down on my shoulder, still in her wix form.

I grabbed a pear and a biscuit and sat on the blanket.

Oh!

I stood back up and opened the cold box again, grabbed the mint tea, poured it into the mug and put it in the hot box with my biscuit.

After a minute I took it out and searched for Perl. She was sitting with her parents on a blanket of their own.

"Perl, come'ere."

She stood and walked over, "Huh?"

I gave her the mug.

"Oh, thanks." She took a sip, "Mm, that's delicious. Mind if I sit with you?"

I shook my head.

"Mother and Father's blanket is small, I can barely fit on it with them," she sat.

A breeze picked up, sending a shiver up my spine. I took a bite of my warm biscuit further pulling my cape tighter, "Brr, I've never liked the cold season."

"Neither have I."

Little Blue cuddled up against my side, Noctua curled around both of us, blocking the wind.

Thank you, Noctua.

"My pleasure, me not feel the cold because of my fur and feathers. You not have fur, and Little Blue's isn't thick enough yet. Also, me like the warmth you give."

After we ate, we continued flying. And flying. And flying.

Eventually the sun was falling and we found a grove surrounded by trees. We made camp and surrounded the fire with our pallets.

This time Alex was twenty feet away from everyone, in the dark.

Something was definitely wrong.

Noctua stayed in wix form and all three of us cuddled underneath the blankets.

TWENTY FIVE

An Old Friend

Woo hoo!" Perl called, "Race you there!"

Noctua and I zoomed to catch up, "Not if we have anything to say about it!"

Kulan was in our sights. We had slept twice and woke early this morning to reach Kulan by noon.

The wind sliced my face, through my hair. Little Blue had stayed back with the others because he couldn't keep up.

We both landed with a thump outside of the town.

"Ha, I won!"

"No you didn't! I did!"

Another thump sounded behind us.

We turned around to see Teamalie and Melodia trot up. "I think you tied, girls."

"But."

"Oh, come on."

"Girls." Teamalie looked sternly at us.

"Okay. . ."

"Fine."

Grimblon landed in front of us, "Wixes need to change form before we go in. Last time the people were a little, well, let's just say surprised." He grimaced, jumping down.

On the way into town I whispered to Perl, "What happened last time you were here?"

She leaned over to my ear, "Someone had never seen a wix before and screamed at Father and Corvus. Corvus got spooked and cawed a few times, making a few other people scream. But after they calmed down, Father explained to the Lord of Kulan what happened, moreover clearing up the misunderstanding."

"Oh my. Hopefully nothing like that'll happen again."

"Elyon willing."

We stopped at the Wheat Inn, it was two

stories high, like the tavern in Wix Town.

We walked in. Except the bottom level was rooms, too, not full of tables.

Grimblon signed in at the desk and gave Teamalie a key, "Your room is twenty six, the same as last time. Ours is down the hall at thirty."

"Alright, dear. We'll get settled and meet you down at the tavern for lunch."

I followed Teamalie to the room with the others. On the walls were paintings and portraits.

When we reached room twenty six Teamalie stuck the key in and turned. The room had a small table in front of a window and two bunk beds were on each side of the room.

"I call top!" Perl ran to one of them and scaled the ladder.

I glanced at Teamalie and Korah, who took both bottoms.
I stepped up the ladder and sat on the bed above Korah. Little Blue jumped up after me, landing at the foot of the bed, his tail dangling off the side. Noctua made herself comfortable on the post, closing her eyes for a quick nap after a day of flying.

"Oh it'll feel good to sleep on a bed." Perl patted the mattress, "Even if it is lumpy." She laid down, her head on the pillow.

Teamalie chuckled, "That's right dear, be thankful for what you have. One of Elyon's attributes he wants us to have."

Thirty minutes later we were ready and down stairs.

"Where's Alex?" I asked, before I caught myself.

Grimblon smiled at me and raised his eyebrow, "He's not coming, he didn't sleep well last night and is going to rest." he answered, walking out the door with Teamalie at his side.

Not coming?

We reached the tavern and a woman showed us to a table, the biggest one in the tavern it seemed, in a more private room.

Mm, what do you want this time Noctua? Baked chicken and carrots? Beef stew and potatoes?

"How about chicken?"

Sounds good to me.

We ordered the chicken, and it was delicious. I gave a piece to Little Blue and a piece to Noctua.

"Hey Eleny," Perl leaned over from beside me, "You want to ask Mother if you and I can go shopping while they visit? They'll be in here for a while."

"Yeah, sounds great."

Perl pushed her chair back and walked around to the other side of the table to her mother. She whispered something in her ear.   Teamalie then said something to Grimblon and he nodded.

Perl came back to me. "We can. Let's go."

I stood and Little Blue followed us out the door.

"So, where do you want to go first?" I looked around, shielding my eyes from the sun with my hand.

"What about over there?" Perl pointed at a little shop.

I nodded as we headed over, "I'm glad you suggested this, I've been needing more stockings."

"I need new shoes, these boots are killing my heels."

Hey Noctua, maybe you should stay out here with Little Blue, it looks cramped in there. With how big he's getting, he's bound to knock something over.

"*Okay, me sit right here.*" She hopped off my shoulder, onto a post near the door and whistled at Little Blue. He sat begrudgingly.

We stepped through the door of the little

building. And I was glad I made Little Blue stay outside. The aisles were not wide enough for him. The shop had dresses, shirts, blouses, breeches, and under clothes, including the stockings I needed. But no shoes that I could see for Perl. I grabbed a few pairs of stockings, took it to the counter, and paid.

"Ready?" Perl was waiting by the door.
"Yep."

We headed back outside, Noctua hopped onto my shoulder and Little Blue started following behind us.

While we walked down the street and I heard a child giggle. *That sounded familiar.*

There weren't anymore shops on this street so we turned the corner.

Wait a second, is that? No, it couldn't be.

"Hey, where are you going?" Perl called.

I ran down the dusty road and came to an abrupt stop when I saw her. *It is.*

"Eleny!"

"Palana!" I ran to her and Omar, grinning.

We both embraced. I looked down as Omar pulled on my breeches.

"Hey, I remembers you!" He said.

I knelt down, "You do?"

He was walking better now, and talking more than when I last saw him.

He nodded and sheepishly added, "You put me in bed at your house."

Whoa, good memory.

"That's right," Palana smiled, lacing her fingers through his thick blond hair.

The sound of light steps were behind me. I turned as Perl jogged up.

"This is Perl, a friend of mine," I said, turning to Palana, "Perl, this is Palana."

Perl shook her hand strongly, "Nice to meet you."

Palana retrieved her hand back and looked back at me, "So, what are you doing here? How did it go at that Jone fellow's?"

"How about we sit down over there," I said, pointing at a bench under an oak tree. "It's a long story."

She nodded as Perl said, "I'll be there in a minute, I saw a tailor sign that I wanted to check out." She went back around the corner.

After we sat, I told her everything, telling her about Jone to Noctua to Raeya, all the way to now. When I was finished we sat in silence.

I hadn't noticed Perl had come up and was

sitting with Omar in the grass. She braided the daisy stems, making them into a crown. After tying them off, she placed it on Omar's head.

His nose scrunched up as he held it in his hands, "This is for girls!" He set in Palana's lap and smiled, "You can have it, Mama, It'll look pretty on you."

She chortled, "Thank you, sweetheart." She glanced at Noctua and Little Blue, "Are you going to introduce me to these friends?"

"Oh, yes. Palana, this is Noctua, the barn owl wix, and Little Blue, a wixen."

Palana chortled again, with nervous eyes, when Noctua hopped onto her shoulder. I gave her a reassuring nod.

Little Blue had been watching Omar and was now laying on the ground, being petted by the boy.

Omar looked up at me and grinned, eyes wide, "Can I keep'm?"

"I'm afraid not, little one. He needs me," I said to him, "and it is enough work for your mother taking care of you."

He nodded and kept petting Little Blue.

"But Palana, what are *you* doing *here* I thought you were going to Meent!"

"We did go to Meent, but it turned out that my family had moved here. We traveled by wagon for a few days to get here."

"Oh, thank Elyon, I was so worried about you! We heard that a raid had gone through there."

"We were gone before it came," she smiled.

Relief flooded through my body, I hadn't noticed how much tension was there because of Palana and Omar.

"Oh, you must stay with me at the house!" Palana smiled again.

"Oh, that's okay, I have a room tonight." I said with a grin.

"Well, if that's what you want, then it's fine."

I heard Perl trying to get my attention, "Psst, Eleny, we have to go back to Father and Mother, they might be worried. We've been gone for over an hour."

Palana gasped, "I hadn't even realized, I need to get back, too." She stood, picked up Omar, and gave me a hug. "When are you leaving?"

"I think in about a week."

"You'll come visit while you're here, you hear?"

I nodded, "Of course."

"Eleny, come on." Perl persisted.

"Bye Palana, see you later."

"Good bye Eleny."

I trailed after Perl.

At the tavern the Bends and Rambeys were in conversation with a couple.

Perl whispered in my ear, "I told you they would visit a long time."

I whispered back, "You also said that they were probably worried."

She shrugged, "What can I say? I don't like to be in trouble for being gone too long."

"Which means you have before, maybe even several times."

"Um, oh look over there, I think my mother's calling." She shuffled over to the families.

I rolled my eyes.

"Alexovin Hendruton to Eleny Nil."

TWENTY SIX

A New and Frightening Path

Alexovin Hendruton to Eleny Nil."
I jumped at his voice. Oh, so he finally decided to talk to somebody.
Welcome.
No answer. AGAIN?
Uh, Alex. . . ?
He didn't answer. He probably didn't even realize he did it, like last time.
But then the cold and dark feeling came. Something was wrong.

I went to Teamalie and did a false yawn, "Yaaaw. I think I'm going back to the inn, I'm tired."

She nodded, busy speaking with the woman.

Noctua, tell Little Blue to stay here.

"Okay."

Little Blue sat next to Grimblon. *Good.*

Once I reached outside, I took off running.

I ran through the door to the inn and up the stairs to our room to think. It was locked. I forgot that Teamalie had the key.

I opened my senses, where was Alex's room?

Do you feel him?

"Yes, follow me." Noctua flew down the hall until we stopped at a door.

Room thirty.

He's in there?

"Yes."

I knocked. No answer. *Do you hear anything?*

Noctua landed on my arm, tilting her white face to the door. Her head shifted left then right. *"Me hear heavy breathing."*

I knocked again. Still no answer. But he was in there. And wasn't responding.

I twisted the door handle, but it wouldn't open. Locked.

Eleny Nil to Alexovin Hendruton.

Nothing.

I tried a few more times, but still no answer. I growled and tried to pry the door open with my Ynit.

Something just didn't feel right. I gasped. I had that same thought all the past week when I first woke in the mornings. I *knew* something bad was happening.

"Me hope he okay. Wait, me going to change form." A burst of light came from Noctua, then she was a wix. *"Step back."*

I nodded and did so. *Please Elyon, let Alex be alright.*

Noctua ran into the door, busting it open.

I ran in the room. Alex was crouched down, shivering uncontrollably.

"Alex! What's wrong?" I leaned over him and touched his back.

He jumped up, pulling out his sword.

"A-Alex, what are d-doing?"

His face was pale white and strained. "Eleny, before he takes over again. I can't hold him for long—"

"Who? Take over? What—"

"Please let me talk, I can't hold for much longer. A man touched me at the meeting in Riverport—"

"When you started acting weird."

"— He was new, and I shook his hand. Something happened when he did and now I can't control myself. You need to get out of here, what he's planning for you isn't good. Deiless is going to protect you, the Bends, and Rambeys from me. I just now am able to take control, but it's taking too much energy. Go Eleny! Before I do something, leave!"

I started backing out of the room, Noctua turning back to owl form.

Go warn the others!

"No, me stay with you!"

You listen right now. He's planning something and you need to warn them!

"Okay, but me no like it."

She flew out the window.

I almost made it to the hall but Alex moaned then his face turned dark.

I ran out of the room, down the hall. I heard the *thunk thunk thunk* of boots behind me, but before I could make it, he swiped his sword under my feet.

    I jumped over it and kept running, "Looks like your training me paid off."

    I didn't make it to the stairs.

    He pinned me against the wall.

    "Ouch," I winced, the back of my head was going to have a bump there. "Alex, fight him!" I looked into his green eyes that were now blood streaked. "Alex, Alex come on! Think! Say Elyon is with me! Alex! Elyon is with you! Alex! Alexovin Hendruton!" Tears started to form in my eyes, "Alex! Please, I can't lose you, too. Alex look at me, I care for you, too, okay? Come on Alex, I care for you, too, I admit it, I was just too worried about my own feelings to realize you're hurting. I love your clumsy self, your loving green eyes, how strong willed you are," Tears were now streaming down my face. "Please." I closed my eyes, "I care for you, too, I realize now."

    "Eleny?"

    I looked up to see his strained face, fighting. "Eleny! I can't control it!" Tears filled his eyes, too. "I can't control it. But I heard your voice, you *do* care? Even though we're of different race?"

    "Yes. But you *can*, you *can* control it!"

    "I'm sorry for whatever I do while I'm under

this spell. Do me a favor and hurt me to get away."

I sobbed, but nodded, "Alright."

His face went stony again and he didn't see when I reached for the Ynit in it's sheath. I grabbed the smooth wood and struck the hilt on his temple hard.

He fell back and landed sitting against the wall.

I stood, breathing rapidly. "Sorry that I listened to your own advice, Alex."

I wanted so badly for him to stand up and say that he was okay then give me a hug, but I knew that wouldn't happen.

His fingers moved a tiny bit.

I took off, scrambling down the stairs, out the door, and onto the street. Everything was foggy.

Wait. That wasn't fog. It was smoke.

The darkness came stronger when the men in black tore down the road in front of me, through town.

I ran down the street to the tavern. I busted through the door and shouted, "We're under attack! Alex is in the Inn, his body is under control by someone bad, please go get him!"

Grimblon pulled out his short sword and

looked at Amon, he did the same.

Other men ran out the door with them. I went in the room where the others were.

"Eleny, what's happened?" Teamalie took my hands, "Noctua said something about Alex, but we didn't get it very clearly."

"He's been under control this whole time," tears started coming again, "That was the reason he was acting weird. Someone who has the Deceiver's control gift has him under a spell. It happened when they went to the men's meeting. A new person shook his hand, since then he's been like this."

"Oh no, not Alex." Tears were forming in Teamalie's eyes.

I shook my head as she sat down on a chair and cried.

I stepped to the small window and looked out, the men in black were gone. It happened so fast.

"It's over, they're gone. I'm going out to see what I can help with." I said, walking out the door, Noctua following.

The smell of smoke filled my nose, there was someone sobbing nearby.

A man was laying down on the ground in

front of me, a wound on his forearm. I knelt and ripped the sleeve off. I took out my linens and chamomile and sage salve. He moaned as I slathered it on, then I wrapped the arm in a bandage.

"Make sure to change the bandage daily."

"I will," he said. "and thank you, young one."

I heard moaning, then saw a young boy lying on the ground across the street. I ran to him, he couldn't have been more than twelve. His breeches were soaked with blood up to his knee.

I pulled it back and grimaced, that burn was going to leave a nasty scar. I put some of the salve on it.

The boy sat up.

"Keep it clean. Don't keep bandages on it. It needs to breath." I stood and kept walking.

People started coming back out of the buildings.

I strode toward the sobbing I heard, then saw her.

Palana was on the steps of a building, her face in the palms of her hands.

I jogged up and touch her shoulder, "Palana, what happened?"

Palana sniffed, "They took him. I t-tried to stop them, but th-the man struck me on the head with his s-stick club," she pointed at her head. Then let out a sob, "I don't know *what* they're going to do to him once they f-find out about his powers!"

I didn't correct her about calling it powers instead of gifts, it wasn't the time. I just sat with her silently, cleaning her wound.

The bloody gash was deeper than it seemed, so I put on some extra salve made of sage for the infection, and basil for the pain.

"He is now in Elyon's hands, Palana."

Noctua landed on my shoulder. *"Now what?"*

Everything went still.

In the smoke filled streets and setting sun, I had a new determination.

I was going to get Omar back.

I was going to find a way to free dear Alex from his human prison.

And I was going to trust that Elyon would lead me on the right path.

"Ooo, me starting to like this plan."

Epilogue

In a dark castle, on the edge of a canyon far away, a man stood at a window. The moonlight lit the gray scar that streaked across his face, down his neck. "Is the Thasfaen you captured here?"

The man's deep voice made the Thasfaen shiver, "Yes, my lord."

"Then question him."

"Yes, my lord."

"And you captured the babe?"

"Yes, my lord."

"What about the child?"

The Thasfaen shuffled his feet, "No, my lord."

"And why is that?" he turned around.

The Thasfaen swallowed, "Th-the Xelman was supposed to capture her, b-but she got away."

"Then get her! She is vital. The Mordens you

hired didn't do it, in fact, they almost killed her! The Xelman you took control of wasn't able to capture her. If you fail me one more time. . ." He drew his sword.

"Y-y-yes, my l-l-lord. I'll r-ready the men."

The man with the scar frowned, "I am leaving in the morning, make sure you keep this place in order while I'm gone."

"Yes, m-my lord." The Thasfaen backed out of the room and ran down the stairs.

He walked through the maze of hallways and down to the lower level. Bars covered the doorways, the stench of mold filled his nostrils.

He went down to the end and looked through the bars at a Xelman and another Thasfaen.

The other Thasfaen was in a corner, the man's blond hair was matted and what he had for clothes were rags.

As the Xelman stood and came to grab the bars, forest green tunic covered in mud, his face became furious.

The Thasfaen grinned at them, showing brown, rotting teeth, "The girl will be captured, she will soon join you both."

Look out for the next book in the series,
Bonded: Reunion and Betrayal

Index

People

Alexovin (Alex) Hendruton (ăl ĕks ōh vĕn hĕn droo tən)

Xelman man. Only known relative: Picklanip Hendruton. Is with Elyon's men. Is a mindvoicer. Age: seventeen. Bonded: Deiless.

Amalek Rambey (ä mə lĕk răm bē)

Thasfaen boy. Son of Amon and Korah Rambey. Age: three. Bonded: none.

Amon Rambey (ā mən răm bē)

Thasfaen man. Husband to Korah Rambey, father of Tsuli, Amalek, and Temmen Rambey. Is with

Elyon's Men. Age: middle-aged. Bonded: Nalis.

Eleny Nil (ĕ lĕ nē nĭl)

Thasfaen woman. Granddaughter of Fenmy Nil. Is a mindvoicer and has healing gift. Age: sixteen. Bonded: Noctua

Fenmy Nil (fĕn mē nĭl)

Thasfaen woman. Grandmother to Eleny Nil. Age: older. Bonded: none.

Grimblon Bend (grĭm blŏn bĕnd)

Thasfaen man. Husband to Teamalie Bend, father to Perlelia Bend. Is with Elyon's Men. Age: middle-aged. Bonded: Corvus.

Jone Samb (jōn sămb)

Xelman man. Lives in Shepla. Helped Eleny. Is a mindvoicer. Age: older. Bonded: Linton(deceased).

Korah Rambey (kŏr ə răm-bē)

Thasfaen woman. Wife to Amon Rambey, mother to Tsuli, Amalek, and Temmen Rambey. Is with Elyon's Men. Age: middle-aged. Bonded: Petechia.

Omar (ōh măr)

Thasfaen boy. Son of Palana. Has protection gift.

Age: two. Bonded: none.

Palana (pə lä nə)
Thasfaen woman. Mother of Omar. Escaped Patera. Age: young adult. Bonded: none

Perlelia (Perl) Bend (pur lā lē əh běnd)
Thasfaen woman. Daughter to Grimblon and Teamalie Bend. Age: sixteen. Bonded: Timna.

Picklanip (Pick) Hendruton (pĭk lə nĭp hěn droo tən)
Xelman boy. Alex's little brother. Age: twelve. Bonded: unknown.

Raeya Pinsa (rā-yə pĭn-sə)
Xelman woman. Lives in a clearing on a mountain near Shadow Forest. Is a mindvoicer and has nature gift. Age: older. Bonded: Mentha

Teamalie Bend (tē-mə-lē běnd)
Thasfaen woman. Wife of Grimblon Bend, mother of Perlelia Bend. Is with Elyon's Men. Age: middle-aged. Bonded: Melodia.

Temmen Rambey (těm-ěn răm-bē)
Thasfaen boy. Son of Amon and Korah Rambey.

Age: baby. Bonded: none.

Tsuli Rambey (t-soo-lē răm-bē)

Thasfaen girl. Daughter of Amon and Korah Rambey. Age: five. Bonded: none.

Zepho Mikkun (zĕf-ōh mĭk-ən)

Jinde man. Helped Elyon's Men. Age: older aged. Bonded: none.

Zerah Johm (zĕh-rəh jŏm)

Thasfaen woman. Lives in River Port. Wife of Lorny Johm, mother of Korah Rambey. Age: middle-older aged. Bonded: none.

Wixes

Corvus (cŏr-vŭs)

Hooded crow tom-wix. He is only two colors, his head is black, and so is his throat, wings, and beak, and the rest of him was a light gray. His beak and horns are a shiny onyx, thick and sleek. Age: twenty. Bonded: Grimblon Bend

Deiless (dā-lĕs)

Nighthawk tom-wix. His beak and horns are a dark gray, his tail and wings are black and on the underside of his wings is gray with one white stripe across each with a few white speckles, just like he had in bird form. His throat is white, his head a shiny brown, his back and legs a shadowy moddled silver with dark browns and greys. Age: three. Bonded: Alexovin Hendruton

Little Blue

Tom-wixen (Bird form unknown). The little wixen's horns, beak, and paws are gray, but the rest of him is a vibrant sky blue. Age: two months. Bonded: none

Melodia (mĕh-lō-dē-əh)

Song sparrow she-wix. She has two brown stripes on her head, and one that went from her eye to the back of her head like a crown. Her beak and horns are gray, and her wings are striped blacks and browns. Her breast is white, and has a few brown streaks, a thicker one in the center. Age: nineteen. Bonded: Teamalie Bend

Mentha (mĕn-thəh)

Barn swallow she-wix. Her chest is a sunset orange, she has a dark scarlet throat, and her back and head were a blue-black iridescent color. Her beak and horns are silver. Age: fifty. Bonded: Raeya Pinsa

Nalis (năh-lĭs)

Red cardinal tom-wix. Bright red plumage with bright orange beak and horns. Black face and throat. Age: fourteen. Bonded: Amon Rambey

Noctua (nŏk-tū-əh)

Barn owl she-wix. Two round, pale orange-pink horns look like a crown upon her head. Her beak is a light orange-pink, too. Her face is white as snow, her chest is light cream, her tail is the buff color of a barn owl, with gray spots. Her wings are golden and glistening with gray spots on top, and on the inside they are the soft, pure white. Age: one. Bonded: Eleny Nil

Petechia (pĕt-ĕh-chē-əh)

Yellow warbler she-wix. Pale yellow with a white ring around her eyes. Light, dull, olive wings, pale silvery white beak and horns. Light brown paws. Age: sixteen. Bonded: Korah Rambey

Timna (tĭm-nəh)

Scissor-tail flycatcher she-wix. She has a white head that fades into a salmon pink under her black wings. Her black tail is split in two, like scissors for cutting fabric. Her beak, horns, and paws are silver. Age: two. Bonded: Perlelia Bend.

Races

Minneckin-

Little person, is one to two feet tall. Their skin is any color of the rainbow, from light red to light purple. Their hair is a flower the same color as their skin color. Their skin glows bio-luminescence. Almost all of them live in Minnek.

Jinde-

Eight to nine feet tall, considering if a man or woman. Very gentle but can be amazing warriors when need be. Most live in The Plains.

Xelman-

Six to seven feet tall when full grown. Very agile. The have pale skin, men have black hair, women have white. The have very light colored eyes, for example, very light blue, pale green, the silver of a clear river, the color of sand on a beach, or even white. Most live either in or around Shadow Forest.

Thasfaen-

Most don't grow higher than five and a half feet tall. They have tan skin and small, pointy ears. Their eyes are darker colors, like sapphire blue, dark amber, olive green, and even sometimes black. They live throughout Iyim except for Shadow Forest and Minneck.

Morden-

Horrid creatures that walk like a man but have fur all over them like a bear. They have fangs and long claws like a mountain lion. They have large mouths and small eyes, but make up for their poor eyesight with their enormous noses that have an incredible sense of smell. They can track and smell things from miles and miles away.

Wix-

A creature with the body of a fox, wings and head like a bird, and has horns of any shape. The older they are, the larger the horns and tail. Once old enough they can transform into their bird form. They have the coloring, beaks, and abilities of the bird they can transform into.

EVE BAILEY is the author of the Bonded series. She loves writing, reading, and drawing, among several other hobbies! She has also published a realistic Texas bird coloring book and LOVES birds. If you want to know more about her or more about the world of Bonded, go follow this young writer @art_by_evey @bondedbook_n_wix_facts on Instagram and @art_by_eve_bailey on Facebook!

Made in the USA
Monee, IL
23 May 2022